SEDUCE

Marie Tuhart

SEDUCE

Weird. That one word buried the bold, explorative side of librarian Tessa Ruthledge until she visits Wicked Sanctuary on masquerade night and runs into Damon. The persistent man refuses to let her hide and pushes all the right buttons, fanning the cravings she's suppressed for so long, including her submission.

Industrial designer Damon Kline wants Tessa in his arms, his bed, and at his mercy. Her spirit, her sense of humor, and everything about her claims his attention. She's the one, and getting past her defenses is a challenge he's up for. This time, he won't lose.

When Tessa's influential father takes on Damon and the club, Tessa must choose between protecting her new family or following her heart's desire.

ACKNOWLEGMENTS

There are several people I want to thank for supporting me through this book:

Laurie, thank you for holding my hand through the formatting process.

Nia, Isabel, and Susannah, thank you for all our sprinting sessions.

Red Quill Editing team, you are the best team to work with.

Publisher's Note: This book contains a dominant male, spunky heroine, and sexy situations.

To My Readers:

This book contains elements of the BDSM lifestyle that are only true to life in this book. There are varying forms of the lifestyle as decided between the people involved. While I researched and talked with people in the lifestyle, this is my take on how my characters choose to live.

If you decide to explore the lifestyle yourself, please remember to always be safe. Never go home with someone you don't know. Attend a munch or a small get-together first to see if this is something you want in your life. Reading about the lifestyle and living it are very different.

There is no mention of the coronavirus that exists in our world right now. I purposely left it out. This is a place for you to escape.

PROLOGUE

"I'll take Tessa home."

Tessa Ruthledge stared at Damon, his dark hair ruffled by the slight wind. She pulled her coat tighter, refusing to consider it wasn't the chill in the air as they all stood outside the bookstore, but rather the intensity of those deep blue eyes making her shiver.

Not only no, but *hell* no. Tessa turned to her friends. Sierra and Crystal always looked out for her. "I'll grab a cab. Don't worry about me."

"Like hell you will." His heavy hand was on her shoulder before she could take a step.

Tessa stiffened and pinned Damon with her death glare. At least, that's what the kids at the library called it when they got too loud.

"Listen. I'll keep my hands and opinions to myself." He lifted his hands in front of him.

Like he'd done last time? Tessa weighed her options. They'd all come from the monthly book club meeting at the local adult store. Normally, she'd go to coffee with them, but she had an early morning meeting.

Her friends watched her. She didn't want to ruin their night. If she said no, they would insist on driving her home and miss time out with their boyfriends. Tessa almost grinned because *boyfriends* was such a vanilla term for what they were.

But alone with Damon? A tremor shook her body. Her attraction to him was something she didn't need in her life

1

right now. Really, though, what choice did she have? Damon was the type of man who wouldn't leave a woman to catch a cab or a ride-share alone. Having him drive her home wasn't that big of a deal, right?

"As long as you keep your word," she said.

"I always keep my word." Damon glanced over at their friends. "She'll be safe with me."

"I believe she will," Sierra said with a smile.

"Damon will be a complete gentleman," Jordan said, glaring at Damon.

"Lay off, will ya. I give you all my word. I'll drive Tessa home, see her to the door, and I'll leave. Promise."

His words sounded sincere, but there was mischief in those blue eyes. Tessa huffed. How long before he showed her he was like the other men in her life and betray her in some way? What the heck was she thinking? Damon wasn't going to be in her life. It was a ride home, nothing more.

Tessa turned to her friends. "Friday night at Sierra's place?" She couldn't wait for some serious girl-time to hear from Crystal about her and Jordan. The drive here with them hadn't been enough.

"Yes," Sierra piped up.

"Let's go," Tessa said to Damon. She walked to the parking lot, leaving him to catch up with her.

"In a big hurry?" Damon said jogging to her side. "Green SUV is mine."

Since there were three vehicles in the lot and she knew who the other two belonged to, the green SUV was a logical choice. Tessa sighed. Logic. How often did she rely on that? Too often. She was tired of making all the decisions, yet she had to. She had no one else to rely on.

Damon unlocked the vehicle and held the passenger door open for her. Tessa used the running board as a boost to get inside. She wasn't short by any means, but this was a luxury SUV.

The soft leather seats held her body in a soft caress, and the dashboard looked like something out of the space shuttle. It put her little compact car to shame. Damon climbed in. The vehicle purred to a start.

"Where do you live?" he asked.

"The apartments over on Olive."

"Nice area." He pulled out of the parking lot and turned right. "It seems like you and I keep getting off on the wrong foot. If I did something that upset you, I'm sorry."

She blinked, then turned her head. He apologized? This man she'd only met twice, who made her feel things she thought long buried, was sorry? Tessa's insides began to thaw.

"I'm sorry too." It wasn't all his fault. "I've been stressed lately, and I guess you were an easy target."

He chuckled, and Tessa's nerves tingled at the sound.

"I know a great cure for stress." He flashed her a sexy grin.

"What?" She'd tried yoga, bubble baths, hell, even meditation. Nothing seemed to work.

"A night of passionate sex."

Tessa opened her mouth and closed it. She'd fallen right into that one. Yet, in her mind's eye, she saw her body entwined with Damon's. She wasn't considering his suggestion...was she? Nope.

"Sorry, no deal."

"Come on, Tessa. We'd be good in bed together."

"We've known each other a couple of weeks, and we've only been together with our friends present. Hell, we haven't even had a first date."

"All that complicates life. I'm talking one night."

3

She stared out the passenger window, not answering him. Crap, she wanted to take him up on his offer. It had been a while since she'd been with a man, by her own choosing. Oh, she'd gone out on dates, but nothing special. Nothing that made her want to take a man home to her bed. Damon tempted her, in more ways than one. But she wasn't going to fall for his routine. He probably used it on all the women he dated. Didn't all men have a line to seduce women into their beds? She'd been burned enough.

Her apartment building came into sight. Relief flowed through her. Damon pulled into a parking spot, and she turned to him.

"Thank you for the ride. And for the offer, but no, thank you." She reached for the door latch.

"Tessa." His quiet voice and hand on her arm stopped her. "I told everyone I'd walk you to the door."

"It's not necessary."

"Yes, it is." He released her and climbed out of the SUV. He helped her down and cupped her elbow.

Tessa pulled her keys out of her purse. The main door to the complex was unlocked, again. She'd have to call the management company…again.

"Shouldn't this be locked?" Damon asked when she pulled it open.

"Yes." She marched down the hallway to the elevator. Maybe it was time to move. She didn't want to yet, as she hadn't found the perfect house. The trip to her apartment on the fourth floor was swift. "This is me." She stopped in front of 403 and inserted the key into the deadbolt.

"Allow me." Damon pushed her hand away and turned the handle, then put the key in the doorknob lock and turned. "It's better to have two keys," he said as he pushed open the door.

She rolled her eyes but kept silent. The lamp in the living room was more than enough light to see inside.

"Stay there," Damon ordered before he disappeared inside her apartment.

What the— Tessa stepped inside her apartment. "Damon, what are you doing?"

"Making sure you're safe."

He strode out of her bedroom and down the short hall to her spare room. Tessa hung her purse up on the hook by the door. She tapped her foot, waiting for Damon to reappear. When he did, she crossed her arms over her chest.

"All clear," he said, striding up to her.

"Why were you prowling around my apartment?"

"Making sure no one else was here." He stared at her.

"What business of that is yours?"

"You're important to Sierra and Crystal, which means you're important to Max and Jordan, which means you're important to me. It's about safety." He kept his gaze on her. "Hasn't a man ever watched out for your safety before?"

Tessa tilted her head. "No," she whispered. Her heart melted a little bit.

"Then you've been hanging out with the wrong men." He ran a finger down her cheek. "Until we meet again, sweet Tessa."

Damon brushed past her and pulled the door shut behind him.

Tessa locked the door and sighed. Maybe Damon wasn't so bad after all.

CHAPTER ONE

Tessa sat in her car, gathering her courage. Tonight was the perfect night for her to see if this was what she really wanted in her life. She blew out a breath, pulled on her feathered mask, and exited her vehicle.

The cool night air caused her to shiver, even with a coat on, as she made her way to the entrance to Wicked Sanctuary. It was Valentine's Day, and the club was having a masquerade party. That was one more reason she'd decided tonight was the night.

Her friends had no idea she was a member of the club and had been for almost the last five years. Her two best friends were going to be mad at her for keeping such a secret. Sierra and Crystal were now members since they'd fallen for the men who owned the club.

Tessa shook her head. It was time. She was tired of suppressing her needs and wants. She needed to let go of everything, and her friends would understand that she needed to do this on her terms and no one else's. She stepped inside.

Goodness, things had changed. There was now a nice reception area, and a man sat behind the desk in a white shirt. "Good evening, name please?"

"Tessa Ruthledge." Her voice was tentative. *Come on Tessa, buck up.*

"Ah yes, Ms. Ruthledge. You haven't been here in a while." He flipped around a journal. "I'm Ralph. If you would sign in here, please." She signed where he indicated. "You haven't been in the club for several years, and there have been some changes. Here's a copy of the club rules. Please read them."

Tessa took the laminated sheet from him and read the rules. She remembered most of them, but there were some new ones. Like the lockers. She handed it back.

Ralph placed a small machine on the table. "If you'd put your thumb on the reader, I'll scan it in so you can get a locker."

Tessa put her thumb on the scanner. The machine beeped. "Thank you," Ralph said as he typed into the computer. "All set for that.

"You'll need to contact Master Max and talk with him about the classes you'll need, and you'll need one of these." Ralph held up a wristband. "You're an experienced sub so pink and white."

The wristbands were new. She opened her mouth to ask if there was another color for not playing, then remembered she could always say no. "Classes?" She remembered Sierra mentioning them, but she hadn't paid that close of attention.

"Yes. Master Max will explain. The ladies' room is the first door on your left. Find an empty locker to put your things in. In case you don't remember, you are not allowed to take anything into the club."

"All right. Thank you." Tessa walked through the open doors and into the ladies' room. "Now this is what I call a ladies' room." It was almost palatial. Lockers took up one wall with benches in front of them. Showers were on another side, along with cubbies filled with towels.

Tessa found an empty locker, put her small purse and her jacket in before closing it and locking it. She liked the thumbprint. No one could get into it, and it made her feel better about leaving her stuff unattended. She slipped on the wristband. Tonight was for her to get her feet wet, once again, and scope out the club.

Smoothing down her hair, Tessa glanced in one of the mirrors. Her hair was pulled back out of the way, the dark blue crop top showed skin but not too much. Perfect. She strode out of the ladies' room and to the doors of the club itself. Lifting her chin, she opened the door. The music hit her first, a low pulsing sound with a beat to it. People were milling around chatting.

She'd timed her entrance to be after most people would be here, figuring she could slip in unnoticed. Pulling the door closed behind her, Tessa slid to her right to take in the differences in the club.

The first time she was here, there had been a St. Andrew's Cross, some spanking benches, and a massage table. The club had expanded. There were stations set up and plenty of them. Tables and chairs filled one small area off to the side of the bar and across the room, and a scattering of sofas and overstuffed chairs around the room softened the look. Another area was a cluster of sofas for aftercare.

Tessa turned and saw the bar area. People were standing there drinking and talking, but she didn't see any bottles of alcohol behind the bar as one would expect. Interesting. There were a lot of people here, which spoke to the popularity of the club.

"Hi. You look a little lost. I'm Regina, one of the club's subs. Oops, I probably shouldn't have said my name since this is a masquerade party."

Tessa smiled at the bubbly redhead with flashing green eyes behind the white angel mask. "Hi, Regina, not lost. I haven't been to Wicked Sanctuary in a long time."

"Welcome back. Would you like me to show you

around?"

"That would be wonderful." With all the colorful masks, she hadn't spotted her friends yet. She adjusted her mask, hoping no one would recognize her. "If it's okay to ask, how long have you been coming to the club?"

"Three years." Regina motioned for Tessa. "The bar area is deceptive. The club doesn't serve any alcohol. It's not allowed unless Master Max has a special party, and it's strictly controlled. But if you want juice, soda, or water, it's available." Regina paused. "The Doms also have space for their bags next to the bar. The green area." Regina waved her hand toward the area Tessa saw earlier. "Usually that's where subs wait for their Doms."

"Usually?"

"It depends." Regina held up her wrist showing off her pink and white wristband.

"What do the wristbands mean?" Tessa never thought to ask Ralph.

"They signify sub, Dom, and experience level. I'm pink and white meaning I'm a sub with medium experience. Same as yours."

"But I never said I was a sub." She hadn't been asked; then again, her application was on file.

"You must have self-identified when you first joined the club." Tessa nodded. "I suspect you haven't been through any of the classes if it's been more than a few years."

"I haven't. Ralph mentioned them."

"They're held on Thursday nights. Master Max will tell you all about them." Regina led Tessa away from the bar. "Around the room, you'll see all the stations."

"It's a lot larger than I remember," Tessa said.

Regina nodded. "When I came to the club, Master Max

MARIE TUHART

had just finished expanding."

Tessa took note of two stations. One with a metal wheel on it and another with a big wooden contraption. Of course there were flogging stations, spanking benches, and massage tables.

"The aftercare area." Regina pointed to a cluster of sofas. "There's lots of seating around the stations, plus, in the back, there's a table with food if you're hungry."

"Thank you, Regina, this has been very helpful."

"You're welcome." A man approached them. "Evening, Master," Regina said.

"Evening."

Tessa turned her head at the sound of the husky voice and froze. She knew that voice. Those vibrant, gleaming blue eyes she'd know anywhere, even behind the wolf mask he wore.

Oh shit, Damon was a member of the club.

"Who is this tasty morsel?"

"I don't know. Remember we're supposed to guess who the other person is, Sir," Regina replied.

He didn't recognize her. That was interesting. Her gaze took in his black pants, no shirt, loafers, and a gold wolf mask. He was the total package, and he took her breath away and made her heart pound.

"That is correct." Damon studied her, and Tessa fought not to squirm. She was dressed perfectly fine for the club. A short black skirt and dark blue crop top to match her blue feathered mask. She wasn't quite ready for fetwear. "I feel like I should know you, but no one comes to mind."

Tessa smiled and batted her lashes. She wasn't sure if her voice would give her away or not.

"If you'll excuse me…" Regina scampered off.

"May I?" Damon asked, reaching for her hand.

10

"Yes." He'd asked. Consent. Safe, sane, and consensual was part of the club's rules.

Damon took her hand. Awareness flowed through her veins. This was Damon, she reminded herself. The man she'd called an ass on more than one occasion, but also the man who made sure she was safe when driving her home. Yes, he made her skin tingle and her pussy clench, but was she ready for such a dominant man?

"Experienced sub. Interesting. Tonight's party is for members and their one guest only. So you belong to someone?"

"I belong to no one." Tessa wanted to clamp her hand over her mouth. "I'm a member.

Damon stared at her. "I still don't recognize you, and I know all the members who are here tonight. Who are you?"

Tessa grinned. "You'll have to guess." She dropped her voice slightly.

"Will you allow me to escort you around the party?" he asked.

"Are you going to eat me, wolf?" Where were these words coming from? Tessa wasn't a flirt, but when it came to Damon, she couldn't seem to control her mouth or her desire.

"Now that is an interesting question." He leaned over. "It depends on what you want me to eat. Pussy or crow?"

Tessa burst out laughing. Only Damon. "You are a flirt."

"I'm a wolf." He growled. "Shall we?" He drew her arm through his.

"This probably isn't a good idea." She would be crazy to hang out with him.

Damon tilted his head. "Are you attached? Were you given the wrong color?"

"I'm not attached, and no, I wasn't given the wrong color." How could she phrase this without giving anything away?

"Excuse me," a male voice intruded. Tessa's attention was pulled away from Damon to see Max wearing a black mask. "One of the Doms would like your help in the bondage area."

"All right." Damon slid his hand down to her wrist and lifted her hand to his lips. "I'll find you later, my sweet." He kissed her knuckles, released her hand, and walked away.

Tessa couldn't breathe. His warm lips on her hand had taken the breath right out of her.

"Now that he's gone, tell me what you're doing here, Tessa?" Max asked.

CHAPTER TWO

Tessa's mouth dropped open. "How did you know it was me?" she asked as Max took her elbow and escorted her toward an area that was curtained off from the club.

"I wasn't sure until Sierra told me." He led her behind the curtain, out a door, and through yet another doorway. It was obviously an office. Max shut the door, and Tessa turned to find Sierra and Crystal standing there.

"Hi." Tessa swallowed.

"Oh my God, Tessa. You gate-crashed the party?" Sierra put her hands on her hips.

"Ummm…"

"This is where I leave." Max leaned over and kissed Sierra's cheek. "No blood." He smiled at Tessa before leaving the room.

"I can't believe you're here," Crystal said.

"I can explain." Could she? Yes, but this wasn't a conversation she wanted to have right now.

"You better," Sierra said.

Tessa dipped her head. "I've been a member of Wicked Sanctuary since right after it opened."

"What?" Crystal's eyes widened behind her green mask.

"I knew it." The purple feathers on Sierra's mask shook with her laughter. "How could you keep that from us?"

"I'm sorry." Tessa held out her hands. "It wasn't something I was ready to share." There was so much she needed to tell them.

"Even though you knew Sierra and I were part of the

club?" Crystal crossed her arms.

"Yes." Tessa's hand dropped. "You can be mad at me. I deserve it. But can we wait until next girls' night, and I'll explain everything."

"Tessa, are you sure about this?" Sierra walked over to her and placed her hands on Tessa's shoulders. "You were always concerned about the two of us with our Doms."

"I was concerned about the two of you, but you both went in with your eyes open, and you had good men to teach you. It's not always like that." A shiver ran up her spine. She'd seen too much in DC.

"Right." Crystal strode over. "Girls' meeting tomorrow. Tessa's place."

"Sounds like a plan," Sierra said.

"Thank you." The three hugged.

"But I want every single detail," Sierra said.

"I can do that." She would tell her friends everything. It was time she let go of the past.

"You do know who the Dom is who approached you?" Crystal asked.

"It's Damon." Her nipples went tight. Damn it, he wasn't supposed to affect her like that. She thought she had trained herself to be immune to men like him.

"She figured it out. Does he know who you are?" Sierra asked.

"No. He thinks I look familiar."

"Hell, I barely recognized you in the outfit you're wearing," Crystal said.

"It's always the quiet ones," Sierra muttered.

Tessa hid a grin. "Should I leave?"

"No."

"Absolutely not."

Those words from her friends warmed her heart.

"Let's head back into the club like we've been in the ladies' room. No one will be suspicious," Sierra said.

"Will Max tell Damon?" Tessa didn't want Damon to find out that she was a member—yet.

"He won't. I'll make sure of it," Sierra said.

"Jordan won't say anything either, if he wants any time with me," Crystal said.

"Thank you both."

"Let's go. I can't wait to see how long it takes Damon to figure out it's you," Sierra said.

"He'll find out at midnight. Remember, we reveal ourselves then," Crystal said as they walked out of Max's office.

I'll be gone before then. Tess had no plans to stay until everyone took off their masks.

"Game faces on," Sierra said as they walked back into the club.

* * * *

Damon glanced around the scene area as he exited. He didn't see the woman with the blue feathered mask. Or should he say Tessa. His cock had come to attention the minute he saw her talking to Regina. He hadn't had a reaction like that since the last time he saw Tessa.

Damon stopped when he found her sitting and talking with Regina and a couple of the other club subs. He studied her. Her expression was animated as she talked. What was she doing here? How did she get in? Wait, she said she was a member? He shook his head. Why didn't he remember her being in the club before? Nothing made sense.

The last time he saw her, he'd taken her home after the book club meeting. The woman had sass but damned if he minded. She was smart, sexy, gave as good as she got, and made his dick hard.

Damon kept his gaze on the women as confusion filled him. Tessa's musical laughter reached his ears in the momentary silence as the music changed. They'd decided to add a makeshift dance floor for tonight, and that meant different music. Tonight wasn't about BDSM play. Tonight was simply a party. Yes, members could play if they wanted.

What he wanted was Tessa in his arms. He strode over to the green area where she sat. The subs went quiet when he stepped into the area. Damon had to fight against taking her hand and pulling her into his arms.

"May I have this dance?" He held out his hand.

Regina nudged Tessa.

"Very well." She slipped her hand into his. He eased her to her feet and led her out to the small dance floor. There were a few couples using it. Damon swung her into his arms.

"So, my beautiful blue lady, tell me more about yourself." Damon kept a respectable distance between their bodies even if he wanted her closer. He needed to play this cool, or she'd figure out he knew who she was and run for the hills.

"Blue lady?" Her voice was light.

"Blue top and blue feathers. Unless you want to tell me your name?"

"Now that wouldn't be fair."

"Unfortunately you're right." He pulled her closer as another couple brushed against them.

"Sorry, Master," the man said, before moving away.

"Master?" Her brown eyes were focused on him. He liked her scrutiny.

"A club title." If she was a member, she should know what it meant. Had she come with someone else? If so, why

16

had they left her alone? "You said you're a member."

"Yes. I haven't been here in a couple of years."

"Why not?" Most here were regulars. Yeah, some went months between visits, but Tessa said years.

"Life." Her voice carried a tinge of sadness, and her brown eyes dulled.

"Did you lose your Dom?" It was possible.

She shook her head. "Nothing that dramatic." The music changed, and he pulled her closer. She didn't hesitate and even laid her head on his shoulder.

Damon took a deep breath and inhaled the scent of vanilla. He wanted to taste her. "Are you looking for a Dom?"

"Are you offering?" There was amusement in her voice.

"If I was?"

Her head came up, and she stared at him. "Not tonight."

His cock pulsed. "Are you saying yes to a later date?"

"Maybe." Her lips tilted up. "Let's not rush."

Her words were soft, but there was a hint of something, not sadness, almost like fear, maybe apprehension. What had Tessa gone through that made her so skittish?

He kept up the pretense. "Agreed. No rushing." He bent his head. "At least not until I find out who you are. After that, all bets are off." A tremor went through her body. "I mean that in a good way, my blue lady. If you tell me no, I'll back off. I don't believe in force." He didn't. While he and Tessa didn't quite see eye to eye on things, she was a little spitfire, and he respected that.

"I didn't think you did."

"The shiver?" She might be dancing with him, but there was tension in her body. Was he really doing the right thing? There was attraction between him and Tessa, but maybe she didn't feel the same way.

"Memories."

He was about to question her more when the music stopped, and Max stepped up on one of the stages with a microphone.

"All right everyone. We've got fifteen minutes until midnight," Max announced.

Damon smiled. "Soon I'll know who you are, my beautiful lady."

"Yes." She stepped back out of his hold. "If you'll excuse me, I'm going to go freshen my make-up."

"You don't need to." His words were sincere. She was beautiful.

"You are a sweet man." She went up on her toes and brushed a kiss over his cheek.

Damon watched her stride away, her butt swaying, and his dick pushed against his pants. Fifteen minutes. Then he could claim Tessa as his.

* * * *

Tessa retrieved her things from the locker, then checked the hallway. Clear. She slipped out to the reception area.

"Leaving before the great reveal?" Ralph said.

"Yes." She hesitated. She couldn't let Damon know who she was, but she didn't want to leave him hanging. "Do you have a pen and paper I could borrow?"

Ralph handed her the items, and she wrote a quick message, folded it, and wrote Damon's name on the outside of it. "If you would give this to Master Damon after midnight, I would appreciate it." She handed everything to Ralph.

"Of course. Have a good evening."

Tessa stepped outside and shivered. She hadn't bothered to slip her coat on. The wind had kicked up while she was inside, and now, a freezing breeze slid over her skin. She hurried to her car and got in, throwing her purse and coat into the passenger seat. She didn't pull off her mask until she was at the main road.

Her body still hummed with need. What was she going to do? At least Damon didn't know it was her, but damn, that man got her engines going and fast. Tonight wasn't for decision-making. She needed to pay attention to the road. The temps had dropped; the roads could be icy, and the last thing she needed to do was slide off the road into a ditch.

* * * *

Damon watched for Tessa to return. It was almost midnight. He walked out to the hallway and over to the ladies' room. "Anyone in there?" No answer. Damon walked through the door.

It was empty. Disappointment flowed through him. Had she fled? Damon marched to the reception desk. "Ralph, did a woman in a blue feather mask leave?"

"Yes, Master Damon. About ten minutes ago." Ralph picked up a piece of paper. "She left this for you."

"Thank you." Damon stepped away from desk and opened the paper.

Forgive me for leaving. I wasn't ready to reveal who I am to you. Not yet anyway. I'll be in touch, Master Damon.

Lady in Blue

So she did know who he was. Why not reveal herself?

19

Did she think he would be angry?

Damon fought against the disappointment. Why had she run? Tessa was a mystery he intended to solve. A shout went out as he made his way back into the club. Midnight. He removed his mask, but it was anticlimactic. The woman he wanted was gone.

"Hey, where did you go?" Max asked as Damon wandered up to him.

"Did you see the woman with the blue feather mask?"

"Which one?" Jordan asked. Pointing out four women.

"None of them. The one I'm looking for had royal blue feathers, and her top matched her mask. The one I was talking to earlier." He wanted to see if his friend had recognized her.

Max looked at Sierra. "I saw her leave," Sierra said. "Sorry, Damon."

"Anyone know who she is?" Why was it so important to him to hear confirmation from his friends? He knew it was Tessa. Tessa with her fiery words and determined attitude not to take crap from anyone.

No one spoke. "It's okay. I'm going to head out. Max I'll give you a call tomorrow." Damon left the club. The entire drive home, Tessa's masked face haunted him.

CHAPTER THREE

Sunday afternoon, Tessa opened the door to her two friends. Sierra and Crystal tumbled in with the bags in their arms.

"We brought provisions," Sierra announced, going into the kitchen.

"I have food." Tessa shook her head.

"We brought all our favorite chips, ice cream, and cookies," Crystal said. "We need them."

"I brought wine if we need something stronger than soda." Sierra unloaded the bags.

Tessa took the extra food into the kitchen, opened the cabinet, and pulled out bowls and glasses. "I'll forgo the wine for now." She might need it later. Talking about last night and the club wasn't going to be easy, but she'd do it.

"All right. Soda it is." Crystal opened the bottle and poured. Each one grabbed a glass and a bowl. Tessa also picked up the package of cookies.

In the family room, everything was set on the coffee table before they took their seats. Tessa curled her legs under her as she sat on her sofa, Sierra at the other end, and Crystal on the love seat.

"We've been patient. Now spill about being a member of the club," Sierra said.

"I joined Wicked Sanctuary four years ago, right after I moved here." Her life had been so different then.

"And you never told us?" Crystal's voice carried a tinge of hurt.

"I'm sorry. I only went twice right after I became a

member, and I stopped." Tessa gave them a little smile. "It was nothing Max or the club had done."

"Why didn't you say something when I first started dating Max?" Crystal asked.

"Mainly because, from what you were describing, I wasn't sure it was the same place. It wasn't until I met Max that I knew." Tessa had played her cards very close to her chest for certain reasons. She trusted her friends, and up until now, she hadn't known how to broach the subject of her being a club member.

"Why?" Crystal asked. "There has to be some reason you kept quiet."

"There was." Tessa shifted. "I trust you two; I want you to know that. It's taken me this long to feel secure enough."

Sierra frowned. "Tessa, what is it?"

"I told you both I lived in Washington DC before I moved here and went to work at the library."

"Yes, we were both surprised to hear you'd moved so far away from your family," Crystal chimed in.

"I needed to put some miles between me and my past. Ruthledge is my mother's maiden name. I changed my last name when I moved here." She blew out a breath. "The reason I did that was because of my father."

"Oh please, not another crappy father," Sierra said.

"No." Tessa smiled. "My dad isn't a bad man. He's made some bad choices. It has to do with his profession."

"Ohhh. Let me guess, mob boss," Crystal said.

"I'm going with lobbyist," Sierra said.

"Close, both of you. My dad is a congressman." While that wasn't earth shattering, her father's political career had shaped who she was today. Something she wasn't proud of at times. It was time to stop hiding from her friends. Who was she kidding; these women were her family.

"That doesn't sound so bad." Crystal stared at her.

"Yeah, well, I grew up with a father whose political aspirations drove everything we did as a family." If they went out, it was always for show. Pictures were taken, her father gave speeches, always the perfect little family.

"Oh boy, that sounds like my family," Crystal said.

"In a way yes. Ten years ago, my father started grooming my brother for politics."

"Is your brother older or younger?" Sierra asked.

"Younger by two years. He's thirty now." She hadn't seen him since she left DC.

"Your father decided on politics for him?" Crystal asked.

"Yes, especially when I finished up my bachelor's degree in library science and told my father I was going after my master's degree." That had been a fight. What had surprised Tessa the most was her mother standing up to her father. All Tessa's life, her mother had been the perfect housewife, never a hair out of place. But that day, she'd taken Tessa's side and told her husband to shut up and let Tessa do what she wanted.

Her father had been so surprised he hadn't even argued when her mother told him they were paying for Tessa's master's degree. A smile crept over Tessa's lips.

"My mother supported me the entire way. I got my master's, and my father turned his attention to my brother and started grooming him."

"That couldn't have been easy," Crystal said.

Tessa shook her head. "My father was running for Congress while I was getting my bachelor's degree. I hated the attention we all got. My brother loved it." She loved her brother, but their personalities were so different. "Allen loved being in the spotlight with our father. I preferred to stay in the background, but I wasn't allowed."

"Why do I have a feeling it's nothing like what we see on TV?" Sierra said.

"Not even close. You see the put together stuff. I hated the back room fighting, the constant press intrusion, and the others vying for my father's attention." Her stomach twisted. The pressure had been on her to be the perfect daughter. She almost snorted at the thought.

"Is that why you left?" Crystal asked.

"Partially." They deserved to know the whole story. "While I was getting my master's degree, I went to work at a local library in Baltimore near where we lived. Luckily, it was pretty much back room stuff so people didn't see me or associate my last name with a local congressman."

Sierra shifted and touched the back of Tessa's hand. "What happened?"

"I met a man." At the time, she hadn't realized how desperate she was for someone to love her for simply being her. "Jack was the sweetest, nicest man."

"You fell in love." Crystal sat forward with a frown on her face.

"Head over heels. In retrospect, I should have taken things slower. I wasn't a kid. I was old enough to pay attention."

"What happened?" Sierra's voice was soft.

"I skipped an important part of the story." Tessa shook her head. "Sorry about that. Let me back track for a moment. When I started on my bachelor's degree, I met a group of people. We hung out together, and one night, they invited me to a get-together. It was a munch."

"What was it like?" Crystal asked.

"It was a simple get-together in a banquet room of a

restaurant. Everyday normal people." Tessa held back a laugh. Her reading tastes had always leaned toward the erotic, and meeting people at the munch had been eye-opening. "I talked with people, and my friends made sure I was introduced to everyone. It was fun and informative. At the end of the night, my friends told me about a small house party, if I wanted to go."

"And you did?" Crystal sat forward.

"I did. It was my first foray into the lifestyle." Tessa smiled. "I was so naive about it all, but I learned. I had really good teachers. As both of you did."

They laughed.

"Anyway, I hung out once a week in the community. I didn't play a lot, but I learned."

"No one hurt you, did they?" Sierra asked.

Tessa shook her head. "Everyone was into consent. When I was comfortable, my friends helped me find a Dom. He was older, but he understood I was new to the lifestyle, so he led me through things very slowly."

"But something happened." Crystal commented.

"As my father's political status continued to grow, it got harder and harder for me not to be noticed by the press, even in Baltimore. My father insisted I be with him and the rest of the family at certain events. Because every event I attended ended up with pictures in the paper, people started treating me differently. It revealed those who were true friends and those who weren't."

"That sucks," Sierra muttered.

"It did. Then Jack came into my life." Tessa shook her head. "Curly chestnut hair, brown puppy dog eyes, always smiling, and working his way up at a brokerage firm."

"He sounds ideal," Crystal said.

"You'd think. We dated. It was nice. I was falling hard

25

and fast. He was the perfect gentleman. Even when he met the family, he wasn't fawning over my father or anything. I thought I'd finally met a man who saw me."

"I'm almost afraid to ask what happened," Sierra said.

"I slowly introduced Jack to kink. He seemed receptive. We went to a party. Jack was uncomfortable, so we didn't stay long. I could understand that. But in our bedroom, he was more comfortable. Anyhow, we moved in together and were seen more and more with my family. The press started writing articles about us. I wasn't happy about it, but I was learning to ignore it."

Well, ignore it as much as she could. The press could be intrusive at times. "Eight months before I graduated with my master's degree, Jack asked me to marry him, and I said yes. It was going to take time to get the wedding together, so we planned it for two years out."

"You married him?" Crystal asked.

"I didn't. It was a couple of days before I was to graduate. I went to Jack's office since I'd finished work early. I figured we could go out to dinner. Jack was talking with one of his buddies about how he had me wrapped around his finger, and that once we were married, he'd have his foot fully in the door with my father."

"Oh hell," Sierra muttered.

"I was upset. I went back to the apartment we shared. I paced around wondering what I should do."

"And?" Crystal asked.

"Jack arrived, surprised to see me. I decided to confront him, and I did."

"He lied," Sierra said.

"No, he was quite honest with me. He told me flat out that, yes, he was using me to get closer to my father. That I was a nice woman but really not his type. I was too mousy, too quiet, and I was sick because I wanted a little bit of kink in my life."

"Asshole," Sierra muttered.

"Big time. His words devastated me. I told him to go to hell and walked out."

Tessa never looked back but had encased her heart in ice. Until Damon. "I graduated on Saturday, and that night, my father was throwing a big party. Not for my graduation, mind you, but for politics." While her mother had shown up for her graduation, her father and brother couldn't bother. "Jack showed up and wanted me to pretend everything was okay. I didn't want to make a scene, but when he tried to kiss me for the press, I lost it." Her face grew hot even now. "Let's say that was not a good scene to play out in front of the press. My father was apoplectic. At that point, I decided it was time for me to get out of the area, and I came out here."

"But why did you take on your mother's maiden name?" Crystal asked.

"I wanted to distance myself from my family and my father's political aspirations. You have to understand, for years I'd met people who only wanted to know me because of my father and my brother as well."

"That really sucks," Sierra said.

"It did. Here I was able to start fresh."

"And we became friends," Crystal leaned over and hugged Tessa.

"We did, and I'm so glad."

"What about Wicked Sanctuary? How did you become a member?" Sierra asked.

"It was about six months after I moved here. We had just met. I heard about the club and thought I'd check it out. I joined, thinking I'd dip my toes back into the water."

"You said you only went a couple of times," Crystal said.

"I did. Not because something was wrong, but because I wasn't ready to go back into the community. Jack's words hurt me deeply, and I started to question my wants and needs."

"And now?" Sierra asked.

"Seeing you two embrace the community and the way Max and Jordan were with you two, I decided to try again. And since I was a member, the Valentine's Day party was perfect, as it was a masquerade. So that's my sad tale."

"It took me a while to figure out it was you, and when I did, I couldn't believe it," Sierra said.

"I told Sierra she was wrong, but then I saw you with Regina, and I knew it was you," Crystal said.

"What gave me away?"

"I knew in my gut," Sierra said.

"I want to know why you skipped out before midnight," Crystal said.

"You two were watching me, so you know why." How could she explain, when she really didn't quite understand it herself? She hadn't figured out why she'd left. Damon would find out soon enough, especially if she went back to the club. Well, she had left him the note. Why had she left the door open? Did she want to go back to the club? Tessa saw the happiness on her friends' faces when they were with their men. She wanted that.

Damon made her feel things she'd never felt before, and he'd barely touched her. She wanted more, so yes. She would go back. It was time to see what the future held.

* * * *

Damon sat down on the sofa in Max's office at Wicked Sanctuary. "Sorry to drag you into the office on a Sunday."

"No problem," Max said, a perplexed look on his face.

"I want to see the log from last night."

"Any reason?" Max stared at him, not looking a bit surprised.

"You know why. I want to figure out who the woman in the blue mask was." His dreams had been filled with Tessa, only to have her disappear each time he got close to her.

"Are you sure you want to find out?"

Damon sat up. "What are you not telling me?" It wasn't like Max to hedge like this.

"Your mystery woman was Tessa."

Damon steepled his fingers and stared at Max.

"I didn't know she was a member," Max said as he placed his hands on the desk.

"My Tess?" He hid a smile. "Tessa who chews me out for saying flirty things to her?"

"Yep."

"How did you figure it out?"

"Sierra told me."

"Yet, last night, none of you told me." Damon wasn't sure how he felt about that. "You're my best friends."

"Yeah, well, I was asked not to." He ran his hand through his hair. "Sorry, but I didn't want to spend the night alone on the sofa."

Damon laughed. "You're whipped."

"I figured at midnight she'd take off her mask and tell you, *surprise*. I never expected her to leave."

Max's explanation made sense. "I get it." Damon looked at Max. "She mentioned that last night. We know all the members, so why don't I remember her?" That still bugged him. While Max bankrolled the club and it was on his property, Jordan and Damon had put in time to help

Max, and he'd made them partners. Jordan and Damon were at the club almost every night it was open.

"I checked this morning. She joined within a few months of us opening. She was only here a few times before she stopped coming—even though she's paid her dues every year—so it makes sense we wouldn't have recognized her last night."

"Especially since it was a masquerade party, and Tessa is always dressed conservatively." Damon paced around Max's office. He suspected her clothing had to do with her job. He'd spied the spicy woman behind the clothing. Now even more so. That also explained his body's reaction to her. Tessa had him tied up in knots since the first time they met over coffee several months ago when Max and Sierra first got together.

"Damon, what are you going to do?" Max asked.

"Go find my woman in blue."

CHAPTER FOUR

Tessa jumped when the doorbell rang. She wasn't expecting anyone.

"I'll get it," Crystal said.

"I'll get us more wine." After her confession, they'd eaten some of the junk food and decided to open the wine. Tessa heard low voices but couldn't make out what they were saying.

"Ah…Tessa, I need to go," Crystal said.

"Me too. Talk to you later," Sierra called.

"Hey wait." Tessa walked out of her kitchen to see Damon standing with his back to the now closed front door, and they were alone. "Damon?"

"Hello, Tessa, or should I say my lady in blue."

Tessa's cheeks grew warm. "I can explain about that. And what are you doing here?"

"I'm sure you can." He pushed away from the door. "I needed to see you."

"How did you find out?" Tessa swallowed hard as Damon stalked over to her, much like a wolf would.

"I knew it last night."

"How?" Tessa barely stopped herself from turning tail and running.

"You're unique and very hard to forget." He stopped in front of her. "I have one urgent question."

"Only one?" She tilted her head to the side, studying him. Was he angry? He didn't look like it. More like a tightly controlled wolf ready to pounce. There she went again with the wolf analogy.

31

"I said one urgent; it doesn't mean I don't have others."
He got into her space. "Are you interested in kink?"

Tessa almost burst out laughing. "I'm a member of the club."

"That doesn't mean anything. The club is nearly six years old, and you haven't been back in almost four years. There has to be a reason for that." He ran his finger over her cheek. "Did someone in the lifestyle hurt you?"

"No." She craved his closeness. What would happen if she locked lips with him? He was close enough for her to go on her toes and taste him. What was she thinking?

"Then why the break in coming to the club?"

"I needed some space." She wasn't ready to reveal her past to Damon. "How did you become involved? I'm guessing Max and Jordan."

"Max, Jordan, and I met at a munch." Damon lowered his head. "I can feel your heat, Tessa. We've sparred and had words, but this is different. You're not spitting and hissing. What's changed?"

There was an explosive question. How did she explain that something inside her had snapped into place when she walked back into the club and tightened when she saw him? A part of her that had been missing now wasn't. The part that longed to be wanted for herself and not her political connections.

"Maybe I realized that you're not so bad after all."

"Oh, I'm bad all right." His fingers slid over her cheek. "Will you be bad with me?"

Yes. Her body shouted the word, but she clamped her lips together. She was so tempted, but they knew so little about each other. "You're skipping a few steps."

Damon froze, and his blue eyes grew weary. He nodded and stepped back. "I am."

Tessa missed him when he moved. Contrary thing she was. "I'm sorry I didn't stay last night."

"Apology accepted." He paced to the door and turned. "Know this, Tessa: I want you. More than any other woman. I want you in my life, so consider yourself warned. The gloves are coming off."

Before she could say a word, Damon opened the door and walked out.

* * * *

Damon stood on the landing to Tessa's apartment and took a deep breath to control his raging desire. Quiet little Tessa was into kink. And she hadn't shut him down when he pushed her a bit.

His body hummed with need. Would he have pursued her if she wasn't into kink? Probably not. He'd been burned before by women who weren't into the lifestyle, and he wouldn't go down that road again.

He'd left her apartment because if he'd stayed, they'd be in bed right now. And Tessa was right. She deserved careful handling. There was a firecracker beneath her creamy skin, and if he wasn't careful, he'd get burned. Somehow, he didn't mind.

He'd just made it to his truck when his cell phone rang. "Yes."

"Hey, Damon. It's Destiny. I've got a family emergency. I won't be able to work for the next few days."

"Don't worry, Destiny. I'll take care of it. You take care of what you need to do, and take all the time you need."

"Thanks. You're the best boss. Don't forget book club Wednesday night. I've got the new selection below the counter." The line went dead.

Book club. Tessa would be there. A plan started to

form in his mind. Once he reached his home, instead of heading inside, Damon went into his workshop, his mind filled with ideas of what he wanted to do. Wouldn't Tessa be surprised on Wednesday when she saw him? Both of them had kept secrets, and some of them were about to come out in the open.

* * * *

Tessa sighed as she locked the library doors on Wednesday. The last three days, her emotions had been all over the place. She'd talked to Max on Monday and found out about the classes she needed to attend. He'd emailed the background check for her to fill out and get back to him. That was something new, and she was impressed.

She'd already done that. The classes shouldn't be an issue either. Damon was an issue. The man hadn't contacted her since he walked out on Sunday, yet he haunted her dreams, whispering naughty things to her. Where the hell was he?

Damn, she'd been without a man for a while. It wasn't like she hadn't dated; she had. But none of the men tickled her fancy the way Damon did.

She tried to pinpoint when Damon slipped beneath her defenses. It all came back to the night he drove her home from the book club meeting—that had been last month. After they'd argued before the book club started, his offer to drive her home had been a surprise.

So had his demeanor on the ride to her apartment. He'd surprised her again by walking her to her door and checking out the apartment before leaving. And Sunday, he'd left without pressuring her. He'd been a perfect gentleman.

The problem was she didn't want a perfect gentleman. Jack had been a perfect gentleman, and look what he did to her. She wanted the bad boy wrapped in a layer of devil-may-care attitude. Tessa shook her head in dismay. Why did she want a man who would tie her up in knots?

Maybe that was the point. She wanted to be tied up. A honking horn brought her out of her musings. Crystal and Sierra waited for her at the curb in Crystal's small SUV. Tessa had walked to work this morning, knowing they'd pick her up for book club.

"Hey you two," she said, climbing into the back seat and putting on her seatbelt.

"Did you finish the book?" Sierra asked as Crystal pulled out into traffic.

"Yes, actually finished it last week. It was a quick read for me." It had been. The book was a little light on the erotic side, though it was still a fun read. "Are Max and Jordan coming to the meeting tonight?"

"Yep, they're meeting us there," Crystal said.

"You didn't mention Damon," Sierra piped up.

She hadn't. She'd given both women an update on what happened with Damon after they left on Sunday. They'd both been surprised he hadn't pushed more. "I figured he'd be there." Her nipples tightened when she thought about seeing him again.

Crystal parked in the lot, and they got out and walked to the front of the shop. Max and Jordan were waiting outside.

"Evening, Tessa, Crystal," Max said before dropping a kiss on Sierra's lips.

"Tessa." Jordan snagged Crystal around the waist and pulled her into a tight embrace.

Tessa looked away. A wave of jealousy flowed over her. She was happy her friends had found men they could love and trust. That was what she wanted: a man she could trust and feel safe with. Was Damon that man?

It was too early to start thinking that way. Hell, they hadn't even gone out on a date.

"Tessa, I have a class starting tomorrow night. Can you make it?" Max asked.

"Shouldn't be a problem," Tessa said.

"I can't believe we're all members of the same club," Sierra said.

"Have you given any thought to who you want your Dom to be during the classes?" Jordan asked as they walked into the store.

"That will be me." Damon stood there with his arms crossed over his chest.

"Oh?" Tessa's eyebrows rose. "I don't remember asking you."

"There's that snappy woman I'm used to." Damon smiled, and Tess wanted to frown but couldn't.

"That's our cue," Max said, escorting Sierra away, Crystal and Jordan following.

Tessa watched her friends walk to where the book club met. "Cowards," she muttered.

"Max and Jordan know not to get between a Dom and his sub unless absolutely necessary."

"We're not Dom and sub. We're not anything." Tessa stared at Damon. He was a little hard to ignore standing right in front of her in a black t-shirt, which molded to his large chest, and black jeans so tight she could see the bulge of his cock. Heat filled her veins.

"Not yet." His voice was soft. "Why don't you go sit down, and I'll be right there."

Tessa snorted, before turning on her heel and marching away. She never snorted. Damon had somehow burrowed under her skin. She took her seat and waited.

A few minutes later, Damon walked in and to the front

of the room where the podium stood. "Good evening. I know I'm not Destiny. She's much cuter than me." Laughter filled the room. "Destiny had an emergency, so I'm pitch-hitting tonight. How did everyone like the book?"

Tessa glanced at her friends, who looked as shell-shocked as she felt.

Over the next hour, Damon did a great job going over the points of the book and telling them which book to read for next month. "If you'll give me a few minutes, I'll get to the counter so you can buy the book, if you choose. See you all next month."

"Counter?" Sierra's voice held confusion.

"He said he was pitch-hitting for Destiny. He must be filling in for her at the cash register as well," Crystal said.

Neither Max nor Jordan looked surprised. Tessa eyed the men, suspicion building in her mind. "You two knew he'd be running the book club tonight," she said.

"Nope," Jordan replied as he stood. "Let's go look around." He pulled Crystal from the makeshift room.

"We had no idea about tonight." Max stood, and he and Sierra left.

Something didn't feel right. Tessa went out into the store. There were several people in line to buy the book and a few others wandering around the store. Tessa walked down an aisle. All too soon, it was only the six of them in the store.

"I'm glad that went well. I was nervous," Damon said.

"You did great," Sierra said.

"Why did Destiny ask you to fill in?" Tessa asked. It didn't make a lot of sense. While Damon had been at the book club meetings, why would she ask him to fill in?

Max and Jordan shifted and were studying the ceiling. Sierra started tapping her foot, and Crystal poked Jordan who didn't respond.

"She asked me because I own the place," Damon said with a grin of a cat that knew exactly where he'd hidden her keys.

CHAPTER FIVE

"What?" Sierra and Crystal said at the same time.

"So I'm not the only one who kept secrets," Tessa said, and Damon winked at her.

"Come on, ladies," Max said, urging Sierra to move. "I think Damon and Tessa need some alone time."

"I agree." Jordan swept Crystal out the door with Max and Sierra following. Through the window, Tessa could see Sierra talking to Max with her hands waving. Damon went over and locked the door and turned the sign to closed.

"So you own an adult store?" Tessa leaned against the front counter watching Damon. Why had he felt it necessary to keep it from her? Sierra and Crystal had been surprised as well.

"I do. Why don't you go look around while I close out the register, then we can talk?"

"Okay." While she was surprised to find out Damon owned the store, she wasn't upset that he'd kept this from her. Maybe because she kept her own secrets.

Tessa went back to the aisle that held the restraints. She knew about the lifestyle, and she'd been tied up with scarves or rope, but never anything like what she saw here in the store. She looked over the boxes until she came to the cuffs. She picked them up. There was some weight, but she assumed that was the metal. Tessa flipped the box over and read the description. Silk-lined cuffs with a leather covering. The picture showed buckles and heavy rings, plus carabiner clips on the rings. Interesting.

"Would you like a demonstration?" Damon asked.

MARIE TUHART

Tessa's face grew warm. "I think that would be very helpful." Why not? It wasn't like anyone besides her friends were going to see them. She wanted to see how they felt, and why not have Damon do the honors.

He smiled, took the box from her, and opened it. Her heart sped up as metal clanked against metal.

"These are a nice choice." Damon dropped the box. "Comfort lined with nice buckles." He undid the double clip from the d-rings and separated the cuffs. He placed one of the cuffs on the display and held the other one. "Now these are nice ones. See this little protrusion through one of the eyelet holes?"

"Yes." She'd seen that on the box and was curious. In all the times in DC, and what little bit she saw at Wicked Sanctuary, she hadn't seen anything like these.

"It's a nice feature where you can add a small lock so the cuffs can only be removed by the one who has a key." He unbuckled the restraint. "Wrist please."

Tessa held out her wrist. The fabric was smooth against her skin. Her nerves fluttered as he tightened the restraint. Heat rushed over her skin as the metal of the buckle was secured. Her breath caught in her throat. Damon ran his finger between her wrist and the restraint.

"Not too tight, but tight enough you can't escape." Then he grasped her other wrist and attached the other cuff.

The cuffs were substantial but not enough to cause any discomfort. Her nerves fluttered with excitement…or was it fear? No. Could it be anticipation?

"Now, by doing this"—he brought her wrists to the front and clipped them together with the double clip—"a Dom can lead you around by your wrists." He gave a little tug, and Tessa fought to breathe.

That little pull weakened her knees, and her pussy

throbbed. Oh yes, she wouldn't mind Damon leading her around, bound for his pleasure.

Her brown gaze met his blue one. Satisfaction blazed bright in his eyes. Did he know how he made her feel? Probably. The man seemed to read her mind at times. She adjusted her arms, and the clips clinked against the metal rings. A herd of elephants stampeded through her stomach. Her skin prickled.

"How does it feel?" Damon asked, his hands on her forearms.

"I can feel the weight, but they're comfortable." She wasn't sure how to explain, but she would try. "My stomach is fluttering; my nerves are awake, and my knees are weak." She didn't mention her nipples ached, and her pussy muscles kept tightening and releasing.

"Very nice reactions. What about your mind? What are you thinking?"

"At first, I asked myself if I was crazy, but once you put them on, my mind stopped processing and went with the feel of them on my wrists."

Damon grinned at her. "Good." He slipped his hands to her waist. "I'm going to kiss you now, Tessa. Is that all right?"

Why was he asking her that? Consent. The word popped up in her mind. "Please," she whispered.

He drew her to him, keeping her bound hands between their bodies, as he lowered his head. His lips brushed hers in a light kiss, once, twice. Her fingers curled into her palms. On his next pass, she parted her lips, and the tip of her tongue touched his lips.

Damon drew back. "So that's how you want to play," he said, before capturing her lips again.

This time the kiss wasn't light. His mouth took

command of hers, tongue thrusting inside and tangling with hers. Tessa sighed and relaxed into his embrace as his hands skimmed up from her waist to her shoulders.

Her bones melted at his control. This was what she'd been looking for…craving. A man who knew how to make her burn for satisfaction.

Tessa started to raise her arms and realized they were trapped between their bodies, she tried wiggling them to get loose, but Damon kept kissing her. Tasting her. His kiss was like a drug she couldn't get enough of.

She shifted as her pussy pulsed. Her fingers clenched. She needed to touch him. Tessa jerked her hands, and his head rose. "Release my hands, please. I want to touch you."

"What if I like you like this?" His blue eyes were dark with desire.

"Please, Damon."

"Fuck," he muttered. He took a step back, lifted her arms, and placed them around his neck, still encased in the cuffs. "How's that?"

"Better." She rested her wrists on his shoulders, and at least, she could play with his dark hair. It was a start.

His lips nipped at her mouth, before moving over her skin to her ear. "You're squirming."

Heat flashed in her face. She was shifting from foot to foot without even realizing it. She wanted…no, *needed* more.

"Your nipples are hard; I can feel them under your top. May I?"

"May you what?" His voice was like liquid chocolate over her skin. She couldn't get enough of it.

"Touch you."

"I'll die if you don't."

"Can't have that." His right hand trailed from her

shoulder, over her neck, and between her breasts.

Tessa could barely prevent herself from pushing her breasts into his hand. Not that she had much room. With her arms over his head and still in restraints, she was pretty much at his mercy.

Fire ignited in her belly and spread. "Yes," she whispered as his palm covered her breast. If her hands had been free, she would have stripped her shirt and bra right off. What was she thinking? She barely knew Damon.

"What is it?"

"We need to stop." Her body protested her words. The voice in her head grew louder.

"All right." Damon lifted her hands from around his neck and took a step back. "What happened?" he asked softly.

"I…" Her lashes fell. "I feel like I should apologize."

"Tessa." A warm finger cupped her chin, lifting her face. "You have a right to call a halt whenever you want." Damon released the restraints and held her hands in his. "Did I scare you?"

She shook her head. Her reactions scared her. "It was me." She fought to get the words out. "We barely know each other."

"True." He released her hands and put the restraints back into the box. "Will you join me for dinner Friday night?"

"You want to take me out?" He was asking her on a date? Why was she having a hard time believing that?

"Yes. I want to get to know you." The fire in his blue eyes was still there but muted.

Tessa tilted her head and studied Damon for a moment. "All right."

His smile lit up the room. "I'll pick you up at your

apartment at six."

Tessa nodded. "I better leave. I do have work tomorrow."

"I'll walk you to your car."

"I forgot. I rode over with Sierra and Crystal. I'll call for a ride-share." She started to fish her phone out of her purse when Damon's hand covered hers.

"I'll take you home."

"But…"

He placed his fingers over her lips. "I'll take you home." His voice held a no-nonsense tone and was so firm that her knees almost buckled.

His Dom voice melted her bones. She'd have to be very careful with him, or she'd end up a puddle of goo at his feet.

Damon turned and went to the counter. Tessa moved to the front door and looked out at the street. It was pretty deserted, but of course, it would be at this time of night. This was Pleasant Valley, not Seattle.

Tessa watched Damon's reflection in the glass as he prepared the store for closing, then he was at the door with her, a bag dangling from his hand. "We'll go out the back door." He pressed a button, and the security gates came down over the windows and door.

"Have you had break-ins?" she asked.

"Not in a while, but this is a deterrent in case they want to try anything." Damon guided her through a door as he turned the lights off in the store. There was a small light on in the hallway.

He opened the door and the gate and gestured for her to precede him. Once she was outside, he pulled the door closed, checked that it was locked, and shut the brushed metal gate, making sure it was secure as well.

"My car is over here." As she got close, she heard the locks click, but Damon was at the door before she could open it.

He pulled it open. Tessa climbed into the vehicle. The smell of leather greeted her. Her body relaxed against the seat as she fastened her seat belt. Damon climbed in, fastened his seat belt, and they were off.

They rode in a comfortable silence. Thank goodness. Tessa rubbed her wrists where the cuffs had been. Her skin tingled, and her breathing wasn't as steady as she'd like it to be. What had passed between her and Damon in the store had set off a string of fireworks in her body.

One kiss and she was a goner. She was attracted to him, but her gut told her this was more than simple attraction. She glanced over at Damon. The streetlights highlighted his handsome face. She was in trouble.

"I'll walk you to your door," Damon said as he pulled into a parking spot.

"There's no need." It wasn't like he hadn't been to her place before.

"There is. Don't argue with me." He stepped out of the vehicle and grabbed the bag he'd brought from the store.

There was that voice again, and her pussy clenched. Tessa waited until Damon opened her door and helped her out. At her front door, he held his hand out.

"What?"

"Keys."

Damn that voice. She handed him the keys. "First one opens the door lock, next one opens the dead bolt."

"You took my advice."

"It was on the schedule for maintenance; they did it last night."

He nodded and opened the door. "Stay here."

Tessa shifted from one foot to the other while she waited for Damon to return. He grinned when he saw her. "All good." He pressed her keys into her hand. "Sleep tight." Damon leaned over and brushed a kiss over her lips. "Go in and lock the door."

She shut the door and leaned against it. "Lock it, Tessa." His voice came through the wooden door. Tessa sighed and threw the dead bolt.

"Night, my lady in blue."

Tessa's legs went limp, and she slid down the door to sit on the floor. This was so not good. Her reaction to Damon was off the charts. Was that why she'd fought with him at the beginning? Was she afraid of the depth of her feelings?

All she knew right now was she was aroused and needed relief. Fishing her phone out of her purse, she looked at the time and groaned. Almost eleven and she had to work tomorrow. She forced her legs to function.

She would analyze her feelings about Damon later. Right now, she needed some rest, but first she had to find her vibrator and fresh batteries. Tessa made her way into her bedroom. There she saw the bag Damon had been carrying sitting on her bed.

Had he forgotten it? There was a note on the bag, so Tessa plucked it off and read.

Tessa, a little something for you. When you're ready let me know. D.

What the heck? Curiosity aroused, Tessa opened the bag. "Oh. My. God." It was the restraints they'd played with in the store. Heat hit her full force as she pulled them out of the bag. Nerves fluttered in her belly. How would it feel to have Damon restrain her and play with her body? To feel his hands roaming over her skin and be helpless to stop him. Tessa shook her head and put the restraints in the top drawer of her dresser, out of sight out of mind. Yeah, right. With a sigh, she pulled out her vibrator and a fresh package of batteries.

* * * *

"Someone looks a little tired," Allie, Tessa's co-worker said the next morning.

"Yep." Tessa smiled and kept walking toward her office. Her dreams had been filled with Damon restraining her and teasing her to release. She'd woken hot, sweaty, and in need. Even masturbating in the shower hadn't helped, and she'd spent ten minutes staring at the restraints in the top drawer of her dresser.

She needed to give them back to Damon. They were too dangerous for her to have in her apartment because her mind kept coming up with fun and naughty things they could do with them.

Ugh. She pushed all those thoughts into the back of her mind. Today was collection development day. She enjoyed acquiring new books, DVDs, and e-books for the library. Sure, her budget was limited, but she found ways to make it stretch. She settled down in her small office and got to work.

"Hey, Tessa," Allie said.

"What's up?" Tessa glanced up from her computer screen.

"There's a gentleman who is looking for a book on industrial something or other, and I have children's hour."

"Okay." Tessa stood up, and her muscles protested. "Dang it, how long was I sitting there?"

"It's almost noon. So about three hours."

"I need to remember to get up more often." Tessa followed Allie out to the main desk. Allie turned right to go to the children's area for reading hour, and Tessa went to the main desk.

A man stood there with his back to her. She tilted her head. The man looked familiar. "Can I help you?" He turned. "Damon." He was here. In her workplace.

"Tessa? I forgot you were a librarian." He smiled at her.

"That's me."

"I'm hoping you have this book on industrial design." He told her the title and author. Tessa brought it up in the system. "We don't have that exact book. I can ask another library for it, but we have others by the same author. Would you like to see the ones we do have?"

"Yes, please."

"Okay, follow me." Tessa walked between the stacks to the back of the library.

"You know, librarians get me all hot and bothered," he said softly.

Tessa stopped in her tracks and faced Damon. "Damon, this is my place of work. Please respect it." She wasn't sure why she was coming down so hard on him. Yes, she was. Her body was already aroused by his presence, and she didn't need to be reminded of her attraction to him.

"I'm sorry. You're right." He looked contrite, and Tessa's stomach tightened.

"Be aware that other people may be around and not understand we have... I don't know what we have." She found the right stack and turned down the row.

"I'd like to say we have a budding relationship."

That was a good word for it. Tessa put her hands on the books. "Here you go."

"Thank you."

"If you need anything else, come to the front desk."

48

She stepped back to get around him.

Damon leaned close to her. "What if I need you?" he whispered.

Warmth spread from her toes to her cheeks. "Behave, Mr.— Heck, I don't even know your last name. Klineman?"

Damon laughed softly. "Kline. Klineman's is the name of the store."

"Why not Kline's?"

"Because only select people know I own the store."

She nodded. "Behave, Mr. Kline or I'll have to go all librarian on you." With that, she marched away with what she hoped was an exaggerated sway of her hips.

* * * *

Damon stifled his laughter as Tessa sashayed away. That was the only way to describe it. His lady in blue/librarian wasn't going to be a pushover. Good. He didn't want that. She hadn't mentioned the restraints; then again, this wasn't the place for that kind of conversation. Back to business, he reminded himself.

He glanced over the books, pulled four of them off the shelves, and found a table.

Two hours later, he came up for air. Two of the books had some of what he wanted. He needed to take them home and see if the information panned out. Standing, he stretched, picked up the books, and walked to the desk.

Tessa sat there typing on the computer. She glanced up. "Did they help?" she asked.

"Two did. How do I check them out?" He set the books on the desk.

"You'll need a library card."

"And how do I get one of those, my pretty librarian?"

Her face flushed, and she glanced around. There was no one near them. In fact, the library was pretty empty.

49

"Driver's license, please." She held out her hand.

Damon fished out his license and handed it to her. Tessa flipped it over, then ran it through a card reader machine. She then looked from the license to the computer screen. "You live out of town a ways." Tessa handed him back his license.

"I do. I like the space."

"So only two of the books worked?"

"Yes." He watched her scan them and print out a receipt.

"Now that you have a library card, I'll request the other book you wanted. It will take a few days to get here."

"Perfect." It gave him an excuse to see her again.

"Are you an engineer?"

"I have two engineering degrees, mechanical and industrial."

"Overachiever." Tessa smiled at him.

"You could say that." He put his hand on the desk and leaned forward. "How about lunch?"

"Not today." There was regret in those brown eyes. "I brown-bagged it so I can make sure I get out of here on time tonight."

Damon frowned. "Not a hot date, I hope."

"No." Tessa leaned back as her co-worker slipped behind the desk.

"Sorry it took me so long; there was a line at the bank. Go take your break." The younger woman waved them away.

Tessa slipped from the stool she was sitting on, and Damon met her when she exited the desk area. "Walk with me?" he asked. At least they could talk outside a little more privately.

Damon wondered for a split second if his grin betrayed

his fantasy as he watched the sway of Tessa's pert ass. His hands itched with the desire to cup those luscious globes while taking her hard and fast. Once outside, she walked down the steps and took a path off to the left away from the parking area. Damon followed with a grin. She stopped when trees blocked them from the main road.

"To answer your question. No hot date. Since it's been so long since I was at the club, I need to go through the classes."

"That makes sense." It did. He remembered Jordan asking her about who her Dom would be for the classes. She didn't need a Dom tonight, but next week? That was something they could talk about at dinner. "We're still on for tomorrow night, right?" His mind started toying with ideas on ways he could crash the class tonight. No, it was better he didn't. Let Tessa experience the first class on her own. He needed to be patient.

"Yes." Tessa took a breath. "Thank you for the gift," she said.

He almost asked what gift and then remembered. "You're welcome." He leaned to where he could whisper in her ear. "I can't wait to use them on you."

Her skin flushed. "I can't keep them."

"Why not?"

"Damon, that's an expensive gift."

He laughed. "Not really." He didn't mention that, with Colby's help, he'd learned how to make those restraints himself. Colby, a member of the club, was also a master leatherworker, and he'd helped Damon pick out the right pieces. "They're a gift, and I want you to have them. This way, when I spend the night at your house we have them."

Tessa's chin rose, and she put her hands on her hips.

"Sure of yourself, are you?"

"I am." He was looking forward to having some fun with Tessa.

"You are so arrogant."

"I'm confident."

She shook her head. "I need to get back to work."

"Before you go." Damon put his hand on her arm. "One more thing. Did you dream of me last night?"

Her eyes flared. "Ass," she muttered as she shook off his hand and marched away.

Damon couldn't help laughing. He enjoyed getting her riled up. She was a spitfire, and he wanted her in his bed.

* * * *

Tessa pulled her car into the lot at Wicked Sanctuary. There were three other vehicles already there. Well, at least she wouldn't be alone in class. Ralph smiled at her when she walked in.

"Straight down the hall, last door on your right," he said.

"Thanks." Tessa found the door and slipped into the room. Max and Jordan were standing at the front, and four other people were seated at the tables. They looked like couples, but it wasn't always easy to tell. "Take any seat you want," Max called out.

Tessa waved and found a seat off to her right.

"Welcome, everyone, to Wicked Sanctuary," Max said. "All of you were at the Valentine's Day party as guests or a returning member." He looked at Tessa and grinned. "You were invited to orientation because you expressed interest in becoming members of the club or as a member have never gone through the classes."

Orientation? Max had told her classes. "We're going to start with the background check and a non-disclosure form." Jordan walked around and gave them each a folder with a pen. "If you have any questions, yell out."

Jordan paused next to her, and Tessa looked up. "Max told me you'd already done the background check, so this is an NDA form for you to fill out so we can update your file."

"Thanks." Tessa opened the folder and read the NDA. Pretty standard. Jordan had probably drawn it up since he was a lawyer. She filled out the necessary areas and signed the form.

Max walked over to her as she closed the folder. "Since you're already a member, I'm fast-tracking you." He set a folder in front of her. "Your background check was clean, as I suspected. But compared to when you first joined, we now have a detailed questionnaire everyone fills out."

"Thanks, Max." He went to turn away. "And Max…" Tessa waited until he was looking at her. "Thank you for not being mad at me. I know I probably should have said something before I showed up here Saturday night instead of surprising everyone."

"You've kept your dues up, so it wasn't a problem. A surprise, yes. Problem, no." He grinned. "But you had your reasons, and it was fun to see Damon tied up in knots."

Tessa chuckled softly. Damon had her tied up in knots as well. She opened the folder and began reading the questionnaire. As she filled it out, she was impressed at the detail. In her opinion, this was a good thing. When she finished, she closed the folder, and Jordan walked over and took a seat next to her as Max was talking to the other couples.

"Done?" Jordan asked.

"Yes." She fought not to be embarrassed. The first time they all played at the club was going to be very intriguing.

"Okay, a couple of things. No cells or recording devices. No photography. No drugs or alcohol allowed."

"Right. I read the rules. Ralph gave them to me on Saturday. All pretty standard."

"Yes. Max said we're fast-tracking you—so next Thursday, you'll be allowed into the club with a Master to walk you through everything." Jordan paused. "The Master you pick will read through your questionnaire, make any notes that he might need to discuss with you."

"That's fine. Who is the Master?"

"You have a choice of whom you want. Me, Max, or Damon."

Tessa swallowed. Damon? Why didn't she see that coming? He was a member of the club after all. "It will have to be Damon." There was no way she could do this with Max or Jordan; that would be stretching the bounds of friendship.

"Very well. I'll let Damon know, and next Thursday, he'll be your escort. That's it for tonight," Jordan said standing up.

"Okay." Tessa's head was spinning. She and Damon were about to go public. Going public at the club wasn't an issue, but it was outside the club she was having trouble with. Maybe after their date tomorrow night, she'd have a better idea of how being in public would work.

"I'm glad you're here, Tessa. Crystal was worried about leaving you out of the mix." Jordan walked away.

Tessa stood and waved to Max as she left. Tomorrow night was going to be interesting, to say the least.

* * * *

Damon pulled the sports coat on over his white shirt. The coat matched the slacks he wore. Grabbing his keys, he headed out to pick up Tessa. He'd planned on calling her and realized he didn't have her phone number. An oversight he'd fix tonight.

Once at her apartment complex, he pulled into a visitor slot and got out. Jordan had called him this morning to tell him Tessa agreed to have Damon as her trainer in the club. Not that she needed one, but it was something they did.

He'd have to talk to Max and Jordan about that. Now that the three of them had women in their lives, they were going to need some help.

The lobby door of the apartments was unlocked again. He needed to find out who the management company was and tear them a new one. Damon knocked on Tessa's door.

"Just a second," she called out.

He smiled as he heard the deadbolt click. When the door opened, his breath caught in his throat. Tessa had left her hair down and was wearing a soft-looking blue dress with a gold necklace. His dick twitched, and his gut tightened. This woman not only took his breath away but caused his libido to wake up and pay attention.

"You are beautiful."

"Thank you." Her voice was soft. "You didn't say where we were going for dinner. Do I need to change?"

"What? No, you're perfect."

She picked up a small clutch and stepped out.

Damon wanted nothing better than to pull her into his arms and kiss the lipstick off her lips, but he wouldn't. Consent was needed. Technically, he had it, but he wanted to make things clear to her tonight.

Tessa locked up and dropped her keys into her purse before turning to him.

Damon cupped her elbow and led her to his vehicle. "By the way, the main door was unlocked."

She tightened her lips. "I'll call them again tomorrow.

They promised to fix it." She glanced at him. "Where are we going?"

"I made a reservation at Pleasant Valley Steakhouse." He'd chosen the place because they could have some privacy.

"Sounds good." She waited until they were on the road. "Did the books you checked out help you?"

"I've barely scratched the surface of one, but yes, they're helping."

"Good. If you need something further, let me know."

"Thank you." Damon flashed her a grin. She really seemed to like her job. "Why a librarian?"

"I like books." She gave a little laugh. "I honestly do. I was pretty much a bookworm most of my life and hung out at my local library as much as I could."

"Natural job for you."

"Yes."

Damon pulled up to the front of the restaurant. One valet opened her door while the other opened his. Damon dropped his keys in the valet's hands and escorted Tessa into the restaurant.

The waiting area was full, as was the bar. "Mr. Kline, so nice to have you here tonight," the hostess said with a smile. "If you and your guest will follow me, we have the table you requested ready."

"Thank you."

"You requested a table?" Tessa's voice was hushed.

"I did. I wanted some privacy."

The hostess led them through the crowded room. The muted voices of patrons, along with the clanking of silverware, filled the air. Waiters and waitresses bustled around. "Here we are." The hostess stopped at one of the high-backed booths in a corner.

Damon watched as Tessa slid onto the deep brown cushion and slid around before he took his own seat. "Your server will be here shortly." The hostess handed them each a menu before leaving.

"Have you been here before?" Damon asked.

"I haven't."

"Good evening and welcome to Pleasant Valley Steakhouse. I'm Victor, your waiter for this evening. Would you like something to drink?"

"Water for right now," Tessa said.

"Same for me."

"Very well. Our specials tonight are the Porterhouse, which can be topped with onions and mushrooms, and our fish selection is grilled salmon. I'll be right back with your drinks."

"They have the best steaks." Damon lowered his menu and looked at her. "You do eat meat?" Why didn't he think about that before now? Not everyone was a carnivore like he was.

"Of all the things you worry about." Her voice held laughter. "Yes, I eat meat, and even if I didn't, there are plenty of choices here."

"Well then, I would suggest the filet mignon if you enjoy a good steak." He folded his menu and laid it aside.

"You've decided already?"

"I come here often." It was one of the best places in town; he, Max, and Jordan ate here regularly when they needed a night out and to talk business.

"I figured as much when the hostess greeted you by name." She folded her menu and shook her head. "I can't decide."

"May I choose for you?" His Dom side sat up. He enjoyed choosing meals for his dates, but not many allowed it. Of course, he hadn't been on a date in a while, but some things never changed.

"I'd like that." The relief in her voice made him smile.

"Anything I should be aware of that you don't like?" He wasn't going to assume anything with her.

"I can't think of anything."

"Is wine okay with dinner?"

"It is."

Victor arrived with their water. "Have you decided?"

"Yes." Damon smiled. "Two filet mignons. Medium." He glanced at Tessa who nodded. "Both with baked potatoes, condiments on the side, with the tableside salad. A bottle of Simple Pleasures Cabernet Sauvignon. We'll decide on dessert later."

"Very good, sir. I'll be back with bread and the tableside salad." Victor picked up the menus. "Our wine steward will be by shortly."

"We have a few minutes now before the server comes back, and I can see questions in your eyes."

Tessa drew her lower lip between her teeth and let it go. Damon wanted to lean over and soothe it with his tongue. "I've never been with a man who has so much confidence. I know I've called you arrogant, but that no longer fits."

"It should. I can be arrogant. I'm fully aware of my faults. As for confidence, it comes with being a Dominant. Although some Dominants are unsure of themselves, especially in the beginning." He'd been unsure of himself when he first started.

"Tell me. How did you get into the lifestyle?"

"It wasn't until I turned eighteen." That had been a dark time in his life. How much to tell her? If he wanted honesty from her, he needed to be honest himself. "I'd recently lost my best friend."

"Oh no." Her hand covered his. "I'm so sorry, Damon. If it hurts too much, we don't need to talk about it."

He turned his hand over and entangled his fingers with hers. "Thank you. I'm okay to talk about it." With her the pain lessened. "My best friend was a big black lab. His name was Bruiser."

She squeezed his hand. "How long did you have him?"

"Sixteen years. My dad got him for me when I was two." In his memories, he could see Bruiser running through the yard to greet him after school. Bittersweet memories. The loss of his dog still affected him, as did other losses.

He pushed away the dark thoughts. "Anyway, I was at college, a little bit adrift in my grief, when I saw an advertisement for a munch."

"Munches are fun."

"They can be. It was amazing how many college students were interested in the lifestyle. We were young though, so basically after the group put us through our paces, we were given a mentor." Thank goodness for that. His mentor had helped him focus his need for control and helped him work through his grief.

"Sounds like an interesting group."

"Yes, they'd been around for a long time and had learned how to encourage those who needed it by fostering a growing environment. Their rules were strict. We weren't allowed to play until we were over twenty-one and it had to be under the supervision of our mentor." He'd learned so much before he played for the first time, and those lessons stayed with him.

"How did that go over?"

"For me, I loved it. I learned more about myself and

who I was than ever before, but it also gave me a family of sorts." It also eased his sense of loss.

"I'm glad." She smiled as the waiter brought their food. "Did you go to college locally?"

"No. I went to MIT."

"Impressive."

"Enough about me. How about you? Where did you go to school?"

"DC."

"George Washington University?"

"At first." She took a bite of food, chewed, and swallowed. "My father wanted me to have a certain degree, and GW was the best place to go, but after my first year, I knew I didn't want to be there. So I found a smaller college that would allow me to get my library science degree."

There was a tinge of sadness in her voice. "Your father didn't approve."

Tessa groaned. "My father has never approved." Her gaze met his. "I don't want to talk about my family. Let's just say, while I talk to them, I will never see eye to eye with my father."

"What about your mother?" Her face softened.

"Mom was the best. She was the buffer between my father and me. She was also the one who put her foot down when I changed colleges and stood up to my father to let me do what I wanted."

"I see." They ate in silence while he mulled over what she told him. He'd question her more about her family later. When the waiter cleared away their plates, Damon told him he'd signal when they were ready for dessert.

"So let's talk about the club and kink."

Her brown eyes widened, and she glanced around.

"As long as we keep our voices down, we're fine.

There's a reason why I choose this restaurant and this table." Damon slid closer to Tessa. He kept his gaze on her face for any discomfort with him being close to her.

"Are you sure?" There was a slight tremor in her voice, and he frowned.

"Tessa, what is it?"

She shook her head. Damon reached out and gripped her chin between his fingers and turned her head to face him. "Tell me." He dropped his voice.

"What if someone hears us?"

She was worried about that. "There's no reason to worry, besides this looks like we're having a date." Her fears were his to ease.

"I know, but…" She closed her eyes. "I'm being silly."

Damon studied her. "I think there's something deeper. Shall I get the check and go back to my place or yours?" He kept his gaze on her to see her reaction.

"No." Her lashes rose to reveal determination in those eyes. "I'm fine."

He kept his gaze on her. No tremor now, just steely courage in her voice. "I reserve the right to call a halt to this talk if I feel you've become uncomfortable." He would do it. He didn't want her withdrawing.

"I can agree to that."

"Fine." He let his hand slide from her chin to her thigh. She shifted but didn't push his hand away. "Jordan called to tell me that you had agreed I would be your trainer."

"Yes. I'm not sure what it involves." Her hand fluttered to her throat.

"Usually, I'd go through this when we met up Thursday, but there's no harm in doing it now." His fingers flexed against her thigh. "When the three of us set up the club, we agreed on some standards, though they've evolved over the years."

"Right, because there weren't classes or questionnaires when I joined. I don't even remember the NDA or background checks, for that matter."

"Yeah, when we first opened, we had only the NDAs. After six months, we included background checks, and two years ago, we started the questionnaires and classes."

"Why classes?" She tilted her head.

Without thinking, Damon lifted his hand and traced the line of her neck with his fingers. Her skin was so soft and delicate. "We found some members were bringing guests who were a little too new to the lifestyle, and they weren't ready for the club experience." He remembered a few of those former members. "So the first class was a basic introduction, as you saw."

"How many make it through the first night?" She shivered as he traced the skin at the back of her neck. "I noticed the two couples shaking their heads as Max talked with them."

"It's about a fifty-fifty rate."

"That many drop out?"

"Yes. I know it sounds high. It mainly has to do with the background checks. Many people storm out at that point."

"Oh, I can see that happening. Some people don't want others to know their personal business."

"Right. We really don't care about stuff like traffic tickets and jaywalking; it's mainly to make sure there are no felony convictions, no domestic or animal abuse charges, trafficking issues, or underage problems."

"Who does them for you?"

"We have a member who is local law enforcement; he helps us out. Of course, we pay for the checks we have done." Damon took a sip of wine. He didn't want her to think they were misusing the system.

"So where does the questionnaire come into play?"

"We were trying to find a way to make negotiations a bit easier. So many Doms were spending hours talking with subs that playtime was limited or non-existent. With the questionnaire, they can read over a sub's hard limits to see if they're a match."

"I wonder why others don't do that?"

"I'm sure some do. It is time consuming, but it benefits everyone."

"So you'll be reading mine?"

"With pleasure." He couldn't wait to see it. Based on how she reacted when he put the cuffs on her at the store Wednesday night, bondage was probably a soft limit.

"And do I get to see your questionnaire?"

"If you like, but I'm more than willing to tell you whatever you want to know." He angled his head down. "I want to be your Dom."

A small groan left her lips, and her body shifted closer to him.

Damn, she reacted to his Dom voice. He'd never had a woman do that before. He'd have to be very careful with Tessa. "Snap out of it, Tessa." He modulated his tone slightly.

Her eyes refocused, and she straightened. "I'm sorry. I zoned out there for a minute."

"What were you feeling just then?" While her skin was slightly flushed, there'd been little change in her breathing. He needed to know what to watch for.

"Warm, fuzzy. Your voice has that quality to it. Makes me think of a tropical night in the arms of a lover. And then—wham—off I go into that cloud of enchantment."

Enchantment? He hadn't heard that one before. Fascinating. "I'll watch my tone then. Thursday night, I'll be waiting for you at the club. We'll take a tour, and I'll show you all the equipment."

"But I've already been to the club." A frown appeared on her brow.

"Yes, but not for years, and I'm sure you noticed how things have changed. The Valentine's Day party was different. There was no real big play going on that night."

She nodded. "All right, so you'll show me around; is that it?"

"For Thursday night, yes. Of course, we'll discuss items on your questionnaire and determine your experience level so I can make sure you have the right wristband."

"That was new. It's going to take time to remember what all the colors mean."

"You'll catch on. They help all members understand experience level, but also help so a sadist doesn't start negotiation with a sub who doesn't like pain or isn't experienced enough." Damon paused. "Would you like dessert?"

Tessa blinked. "Why not. Some coffee too, please."

Damon signaled the waiter and ordered dessert with coffee. When he turned back to Tessa, her fingers were tapping on the table. Was she nervous? Or impatient?

"What else would you like to know?"

"What happens after Thursday? Jordan said you'd be my trainer."

"Yes. I will stay with you in the club. If you choose to play with me, that's fine. If not, I can find you a Dom who matches your criteria." It would kill him to find someone else for her to play with, but he'd do it. It had to be her choice.

64

"You wouldn't mind finding me someone else?" Her question was soft, but her fingers stopped moving. Good sign? Maybe.

"I wouldn't be happy, but this isn't about me; it's about you." Her eyes widened. "I mean that, Tessa. A bonded Dom/sub relationship is something special. One I've never had."

"But you think I'm the right one?"

"Yes." He wasn't going to lie or hide anything. "From the first time we met, there was a spark." He couldn't deny it. Damon would make sure he kept her safe. He wouldn't lose her as he'd lost in the past.

"A spark of annoyance."

Damon chuckled. "You are easy to provoke at times."

"And you're very good at doing that," she snapped back.

There was his spunky woman. "I mean what I say. If you need a contract between us, I can have it arranged."

Tessa pursed her lips. "No, I don't need a contract." She took a breath. "I believe Max and Jordan would have your head if you did something you weren't supposed to."

"Not to mention Sierra and Crystal."

Her laughter lightened the mood. "My friends are the best."

"They are, and I'm glad they're looking out for you. Tell me how you got involved with kink."

"Much like you, in college at a munch. But it was a different time then." She stopped as the waiter arrived with their dessert and coffee.

A large piece of chocolate cake with a fork was placed on the table and their coffee poured.

"Dessert." Damon lifted the fork, cut a piece, and held it to Tessa's lips. Her cheeks flushed as she parted her lips and allowed him to slip the bite into her mouth. The fork moved as she brushed her tongue over it.

Damon slowly pulled the fork from her mouth, watching as she closed her eyes and savored the burst of chocolate on her tongue. His cock stiffened, and he made a mental note about food play being a possibility.

Tessa's lashes rose, and her cheeks bloomed even more when she realized he was watching her. "That is delicious, but I can feed myself." She went to reach for a fork only to realize there was only one.

"It's my pleasure to feed you." Damon took a small bite before getting another piece on the fork for Tessa. When he held it out to her, she hesitated, then opened her mouth for the treat. Each time he gave her a bite, his dick pulsed and hardened.

Their coffee had gone cold by the time the cake was finished. Damon signaled the waiter for fresh cups.

"So tell me how your first munch went."

"It was nice. A bunch of us from the university were there, and the people were nice. We were all over twenty-one." She took a sip of her coffee. "I hit it off with several people and got invited to a private party."

Damon frowned. "Private parties can be dangerous for someone new."

"I was lucky. The people at the munch took me under their wing and made sure I was safe. I will say that party was eye-opening."

"Did you play?"

"A little, not that night. A couple of years later, a small club opened, and we all went. My friends found me a Dom. He was older and understood I was new to the lifestyle. He took good care of me, never pushing me and helping me understand."

"How old were you when you found your Dom?"

"Twenty-five."

Not too young. "Why did you wait four years?"

"Because I never felt comfortable at some of the house parties. My friends and I never went to one without each other, and we all left together."

Damon said a silent prayer of thanks that she'd had good people around her. "When and why did you stop coming to Wicked Sanctuary?"

"I moved here a little over four years ago and joined the club on recommendation of my Dom from DC. The club has changed so much from the first time I saw it."

Damon nodded. "It has. As we increased membership, we saw ways to make things better."

"Anyway, I went to the club twice and stopped." Her fingers toyed with the rim of her coffee cup. "It wasn't anything that happened at the club or anything. It was me. I needed a break to find myself."

"And did you find yourself?"

"I thought so. Until Sierra and Crystal started going to the club." Her lips turned up. "The conversations at girls' night made me realize I'd cut a part of myself off."

"Why the Valentine's Day party?"

"Anonymity." She pushed the cup away. "I wanted to see for myself what the club had become, and having a masquerade party helped me do that without tipping anyone off, or so I thought."

"Why didn't you say anything to me?" He was curious why she didn't tell him she'd recognized him. Some men might have been angry. He might have been for a few minutes, but then he had a feeling Tessa had good reasons for what she did. And, to be honest, he'd been completely under her spell that night.

67

"At first, I was surprised to see you there. I mean, I knew you were friends with Max and Jordan but didn't realize you were into the lifestyle. After that, I thought, what the heck. How did you figure out it was me?"

"There was something too familiar about you. Plus your voice." He gave her a lopsided grin. "How did you know I was the Dom behind the wolf mask?"

She glanced down at the table and then back at him, her eyes alight with mischief. "The way you held yourself, your voice and...I knew."

"You never let on." He'd seen a woman he wanted to play with that night. He was standing on the cusp of something special. He'd finally found a woman who called to his inner Dom. Tessa reacted to him without thought.

Surprise smacked him upside the head. They were already good together. When they played, it was going to be epic. He was ready to step off the cliff into a full-fledged relationship with Tessa. Who could have guessed it would happen to him so quickly?

"You left before midnight? I looked all over for you." He couldn't keep the disappointment out of his voice.

"I'm sorry." She ducked her head again.

Damon studied her. "But you left me a note. That's when I realized you knew who I was. I'm glad you left it."

"I didn't want you to think I ran out because of you. It was more me. I wasn't ready for anyone else to know who I was."

"What aren't you telling me?"

"Let's say my family is in the spotlight a lot, and it's taught me to be very careful."

"Care to elaborate?" He wondered what her family was involved with? Politics? Lobbyist? Something else? There were a hundred choices.

"Not tonight."

Damon let it go. He'd get the full story out of her another night. "I'll give you some time, but I need the full story."

"What about yours?"

"What do you mean?"

"You said you got into kink in college, but never told me how you came to be a partner in Wicked Sanctuary."

"I didn't." He glanced at his watch. "How about we save that for another night. It's almost ten, and I believe you have to work tomorrow?"

"And how do you know that?" Her eyes narrowed.

Damon signaled the waiter for the check. "I asked a little birdie." Once he'd paid for their meal, he escorted Tessa to his car. The ride was silent, and he wondered what Tessa was thinking. When they arrived, she waited for him to open her door and didn't say anything when he escorted her up to her apartment. She even handed him her keys.

"Thank you," he said.

"I don't want to argue with you."

"I appreciate that." He opened the door and slipped inside, checking the rooms quickly. "All clear."

"Why do you check my apartment?" She dropped her keys and purse on the table by the front door.

"Safety."

"Really?" She tilted her head. "I think it's a control issue."

His lips tilted up. "I want to make sure you're safe." Damon lifted his hand and trailed his fingers over her cheek before curving his hand behind her neck. "I want to kiss you."

"I want that too." She lifted her face to his.

He captured her lips.

69

A sigh left her mouth, and his tongue delved in. He tasted the barest hint of coffee. His dick pulsed.

Tessa's arms encircled his neck as his free hand curved around her waist and pulled her to him, her body soft against his hardness. He wanted more. More than a kiss.

She shifted, and her pert nipples pressed against his chest. Damon barely restrained the need inside him to do more than kiss her. It wasn't time yet.

He lifted his head. Her eyes were dreamy, and her lips red from his kiss. "I want to tumble you into bed," he whispered.

Tessa didn't reply, but she didn't move away from him either. She was going to be the death of him. Mustering up every ounce of control he had, Damon released her neck and took a step back.

"No," she whispered.

"Yes, sweetheart." He took a deep breath, then took another step back. "It's too soon, no matter what my body wants."

"Mine wants it too." Her hands fluttered to his chest.

"Another night." He captured her wrists and pulled her hands away from his heated body. "Are you free on Sunday?"

"I have an early meeting Monday so I can't be out late."

"How about lunch? I'll pick you up at noon."

"I can do that." Her eyes were clear and focused.

"All right. I'll tell you more about myself and the club then, and we can go over your questionnaire together. In private."

Color bloomed in her cheeks.

"Good night." He leaned down and brushed another kiss over her soft lips, before releasing her and stepping out the door. Damon reached back and pulled the door shut. He waited until he heard the locks click and made his way down the hall with a spring in his step.

Sunday. Maybe a picnic lunch at his house. Plans started swirling in his head. Tonight had gone well, and he was delighted even if he did have a hard-on that wasn't going to be satisfied until he bedded Tessa.

CHAPTER SIX

Tessa tossed yet another outfit on her bed. What the hell was she going to wear? Saturday had passed in a blur of work and thinking about Damon. Now it was eleven on Sunday, and she still couldn't pick out an outfit to wear.

He'd said picnic. Jeans would be practical, but which ones. Blue, stone washed, black, tan...ugh...she wanted to pull her hair out. Her cell rang, and she glanced at the display. Sierra.

"Hey, Sierra," she said as she answered the phone.

"So, heard you went to dinner with Damon Friday night."

"I did, and do you have time to video chat?"

"Is everything okay?" The worry in Sierra's voice was evident.

"It's fine. I need some help."

"Sure." A second later, Sierra's face appeared. "What do you need help with?"

"Damon is picking me up for a picnic lunch in less than an hour. I can't figure out what to wear."

Sierra giggled. "Jeans would be good."

"Funny. What color?"

"You have way too many choices. Put on a pair of blue jeans."

Tessa grabbed a pair and put them aside. "Top?"

"Let's see...show me your closet." Tessa turned the camera toward her closet. "The blue-black one with the design on the sleeve."

"I forgot I bought this." She pulled the blouse out.

"What am I thinking? It's February. How are we going to have a picnic?"

"It's not snowing," Sierra offered.

"No, but it's not warm enough to be outside either."

"True, the temp is forty out. A little cold for a picnic." There was another voice in the background. "Be right there, honey."

"I better let you go." Tessa rubbed her forehead.

"Don't stress out. Wear the outfit, I'm sure Damon has something special in mind. Bye." The screen went blank.

Tessa sighed and grabbed her clothing. A picnic in February. What was Damon thinking?

There was a knock at her front door on the dot of noon. She looked out to make sure it was Damon before opening it. The building lock was still broken; she'd complained again yesterday.

"Hi," she said.

"Hello, beautiful." Damon leaned down and brushed a kiss over her cheek. "Nice outfit."

"Thank you, but isn't it a little cold out for a picnic?"

"It is, but I have a special place in mind. As long as you're okay with being alone with me at my home?"

There was that consent again. Tessa's insides melted. "I'm fine with it." She reached back for her jacket and purse.

"Let me." Damon took her jacket from her and held it out.

"Such a gentleman," Tessa commented.

"I try."

She pulled the door shut behind her and locked it, and they were on their way. "How far out of town do you live?" Tessa asked as he drove.

"On the outskirts. I'm not as far out as Max."

"Why out there?" There wasn't a lot of housing in that area.

"I needed space for my other business."

"What do you do besides run the bookstore? I know you have degrees in engineering." Until he said that, she'd forgotten she didn't know what he did for a living, but he said he'd gone to MIT and picked up some industrial engineering books at the library.

"Mechanical and electrical engineering." He turned down a small paved road.

"Those are your degrees. Not what you do." The trees were beautiful this time of year. The fir and pine trees are so green. If a winter storm came in they would be covered with snow. Tessa shivered.

"Cold?"

"No. I was thinking how the trees would look when it snowed."

"They're beautiful, but the snow makes driving a little hard."

"I bet. I..." Her voice trailed off as the road opened up and a beautiful home came into view.

It was a single story, somewhat modern home. There were angled roofs with intricate carvings on the archways. Wood-looking columns. Green grass and shrubs and trees that would bloom come spring.

"It's gorgeous," she whispered as Damon pulled up the stone driveway.

"Thank you." He pressed a button, and the garage door opened. He pulled inside. "It will be warmer this way."

Damon was there when she opened her door. "Normal garage," he said.

"It's warm."

"I had it insulated when I had the house built. Keeps

74

SEDUCE

the cars warmer in winter." He unlocked a door and opened it. "Utility room." He flipped the lights on.

The tile was a beige color, and a front loading washer and dryer were off to one side, white cabinets above. On the other side were more cabinets with a place to fold laundry and a small bench with baskets beneath it.

"This is very nice." She'd kill for a laundry room like this.

"I like it." He shut the door to the garage and slipped off his shoes. "If you don't mind slipping off your shoes?"

Tessa was glad she wore her sneakers. She slipped them off and set them in an empty basket. Damon, she noticed, placed his boots in one of the cabinets.

"There's slippers in the other basket," he said as he straightened.

"I'm fine."

"All right. He reached past her and opened the door to the house. "Welcome to my home."

"Thank you."

"I'll give you the tour, then we can have our picnic." He guided her into the house and down the short hallway. The hardwood gleamed under her feet. No wonder he'd wanted her to take her shoes off.

"Off to your left is technically the study, but I use it as a library."

"Oh?" She looked in the door. The walls were lined with bookcases. In the middle of the room sat a leather chair with a small table next to it. Her tummy turned over in anticipation of being able to check out his library. "Very cozy."

"I figured you'd appreciate that." His eyes gleamed as he guided her into the open area of his home. "Guest bedrooms on the other side of the family room down that hall. Master bedroom over there." He pointed to a door on the left. "Then we have the formal dining room off a little behind us, and this is the family room and kitchen." He waved his hand to the left.

Tessa's breath caught when she saw his kitchen. The gleaming stainless steel appliances, a six-burner gas stove. Light brown marble counter tops with a stone-looking backsplash. "Very nice kitchen."

"I like to cook now and again."

Tessa followed him deeper into the family room and stopped. The breakfast bar stone was like the outside of an old English cottage. She turned and saw the fireplace had the same type of look. "I love the granite."

"I wanted that rustic look." He flashed her a grin. "I bet you're wondering how we're going to do this picnic?"

"It did cross my mind." His house was beautiful, and it fit Damon. Not too modern, but fit his style.

"Then let me show you." He led her to the small nook area she hadn't noticed before and opened the door to go outside into the backyard.

"Oh my." Tessa stepped out onto the lanai. The sides fully enclosed in glass, with high wooden beams and roof. The room was warm. A table and chairs were pushed up against one side, and in the middle of the lanai, a blanket had been spread on top of a super thick area rug. "This is beautiful."

She circled the lanai and looked out the glass. Off to one side was a barbecue inlaid with the same granite as inside the house, along with a fireplace. A large wicker table and chairs were covered with heavy plastic sheeting. Outside the center glass door were granite steps down to another patio and a covered pool. "You have a pool?"

"Yes." He came up behind her. "It's nice to have

during the summer and great exercise."

"Like you need exercise."

He laughed. "Make yourself comfortable, and I'll go get our picnic."

"Can I help?"

Damon regarded her for a moment. "Let me take care of you today. Can you do that?"

Surprise hit Tessa's blood stream at his words. "I think so." It was an honest answer. He smiled and disappeared back into the house. Tessa stared out at the view. The rolling hills were soothing.

She turned when she heard the door open. Damon stepped out with a large basket and a couple bottles of water. Tessa started to help him, and he glared at her. Okay, the man was serious about taking care of her.

"Come sit down." He set the basket and water on the blanket, holding his hand out to her.

Tessa put her hand in his, and he helped her to the ground before he knelt and unloaded the basket. Skewers of chicken and veggies, tiny sandwiches, a plate of bite-sized fruit, and another plate of cheese and crackers. Then plates and utensils.

"Dessert is in the fridge," he said, setting the basket aside.

"This all looks delicious."

"The sandwiches are ham and cheese or turkey and cheese." He held up a plate. "What would you like?"

"How about a little bit of everything."

"Sounds good." Using tongs, he placed two sandwiches on her plate, along with two skewers of chicken, some fruit, and some cheese and crackers. He held the full plate out to her. Tessa took it and waited until he'd served himself before she picked up a sandwich.

The flavors flowed over her taste buds. Honey mustard along with mayo. She wiped her fingers on the napkin. "That is so good. What kind of cheese?"

"That one has mozzarella. There's Swiss and cheddar on the others."

"And the turkey?"

"Cheddar or American, smoked turkey with a mayo and a light cranberry spread."

Tessa's stomach growled. She picked up the chicken skewer and pulled a piece of chicken off to pop in her mouth. She groaned in ecstasy.

"Good?" he asked with a grin.

"Did you marinate the chicken?" She couldn't quite put her finger on the flavors.

"I did."

Tessa waited for him to continue. She'd never experienced flavors like this.

"Mixture of soy sauce, rice wine vinegar, honey, peanut and sesame oil, garlic, onion, and a little bit of ginger."

"I'll have to try that." She was always on the lookout for new ways to cook chicken. Or easy ways to cook chicken. She was helpless in the kitchen.

"I have lots of recipes."

"Is that an offer to share?" Where did that come from?

"Depends on what you'll give me for them." He gave her a grin.

Her core tightened. Damn, he was sexy. Tessa tilted her head and thought for a minute. "A kiss."

He smiled. "One for each recipe."

She laughed. "Trying to take advantage, are we?" She was getting better at flirting with him.

"Only if you'll let me."

They finished eating, and Damon cleared everything away. "I had Max email me your questionnaire."

Heat rushed to Tessa's cheeks. "Okay." It was hard to take a breath. Yes, she wanted Damon to be her trainer, but at the same time, this was scary.

"Would you like to read my questionnaire?"

"You'd let me?" That was surprising.

"Of course. You have a right to know who you're playing with. Or I'm more than willing to tell you whatever you want to know."

She was impressed. "I'd like to read it. It's not because I don't trust you; I do. I'd like to see how we compare."

He inclined his head. "I'll have Max email mine to you. I looked yours over. We're very compatible. But I do have some questions."

"All right." Putting her fears aside, Tessa tried to relax. She was ready to do this.

"It's mainly around the toy section. The one about beads or balls insertion, you said vaginally only and a hard limit on butt plugs."

"I'm not ready to do anything anal." She shivered.

"That's fine. Is it something maybe at a later date you're willing to try?"

"Maybe." She wasn't sure she would ever be ready. Anal play had looked painful to her the few times she witnessed it.

"All right. You didn't circle hard or soft limit on toys in public when under clothing."

"I need more clarification on that." She was aware of the statement, but she wanted to hear from him what his thoughts were.

"For me, it would mean, maybe a wireless vibrating bullet I put in you and turn on and off at a restaurant or party. Or vibrating panties."

"Oh?" She'd seen a lot in DC, including women who wore vibrating nipple rings under their clothing. You'd think people in the political eye would be more circumspect, but they weren't. Well, probably most people outside the lifestyle wouldn't notice or, if they did, even know what they were.

"What's bothering you?"

Tessa shifted on the blanket. "I'm fine playing in public at the club, but not anywhere else." That was really it. She'd been under media scrutiny for so long, she still lived in fear they'd find her, and it would be a shit show. Past betrayals still weighed heavily on her mind.

"I can live with that. What about playing here at my home or your apartment?"

"As long as we're discreet, I'm fine with it."

"You don't seem to mind being seen at the store or the book club."

She shifted again. "That's different. I'm really there for the book club and nothing else." But she did look around the other night. She needed to be more careful. Yes, it had been years since the press followed her around, but that didn't mean they wouldn't start again if they figured out where she was and who she was.

Heck, that reporter had hounded Jordan and Crystal about their case. It wasn't something Tessa wanted to deal with again. She needed her privacy.

"Interesting." He grabbed a pillow and lay back on the blanket and turned his head so he could see her. "How do you feel about being my sub?"

Instant heat flowed through her veins at his words. "Shouldn't we go through the training program first?" Chicken.

"We can but think about how much more fun we can have." Damon turned on his side and ran his hand over her denim-clad leg. Nerves came alive under his touch. "And it's not really training. With brand new members, we have the class you went through the other night for the background checks, questionnaire, etc. Class two is going over rules and protocols. Class three is introduction to the club and answering questions. And class four is a night to play, depending on experience level."

"Talk to me about that. How do you determine experience levels?" She was interested in their concept.

"The questionnaire helps. We can usually tell right away when someone is very new to the lifestyle, wants to explore more, or has been in the lifestyle." His fingers trailed up her leg to her knee. "When rules and protocols come into play, novices need a lot of explanation, whereas others don't."

"But rules and protocols are not the same in each club?"

"You are correct." His finger traced circles on her kneecap. "Ours are pretty basic and detailed in the documentation. You did read what you were given, right?"

"I did." She had read the rules, which were pretty straightforward. The protocols were fairly simple as well. "Tell me more about the wristbands."

"Those were my idea." He scooted closer to her. "I'd noticed a lot of time was being wasted on negotiation, not that it isn't important. It is. But some Doms and subs were spending hours talking and had no time to see if they played well together." He walked his fingers up to her thigh.

"So how do the wristbands work?" Tessa tried to ignore Damon's touch, but it was hard.

"We read over the questionnaire of the sub, and we go

with a color system. White is for a new subs."

"But, technically, I'm not new."

"You're not."

"Okay, go on."

"Pink and white is a medium experience sub. Green and white, experienced. Red and white for a masochist. Lastly purple and white for a taken sub."

"What about the Doms?"

"Masters/Doms are black, DM is yellow, Red is for sadist."

"Isn't that a little confusing that Masters and Dom are both black wristbands?"

Damon's eyes widened. "We hadn't thought about that, but now that you mention it, it could be. I'll have to bring that up with Max and Jordan."

"I noticed they were an elastic band with fabric over it. Don't they get caught on things?"

"Observant, aren't you." He ran his finger over her cheek.

Heat flooded Tessa's face. Damon's touch was so soft, so sensual.

"They do sometimes. We're working on a new band that will be less likely to catch," he said.

"It's good because it allows the Doms to see if a sub fits their criteria before they even talk to them. More places should use that."

Damon smiled. "So talk to me more. What would you like to do in the club?"

He shifted even closer to her, and his body heat called to her.

Tessa shifted. "I need to move; my legs are falling asleep."

Damon sat up. "Here." He helped her into a better

position. "Now lay back."

Tessa did as he said. "Oh." He positioned her so when she laid back, her head was on his stomach.

"Better?" he asked.

"Yes." This was intimate, but not too intimate. Or was it? Her head rested on him. Tessa shrugged away her concerns. She closed her eyes and thought for a moment about his question about what she would like to do in the club. "I like different things."

"What have you done before? From the way you reacted to the restraints, I'm thinking you've done bondage before."

"No. Bondage wasn't something I was interested in. Until you." Her hand fluttered to her chest when she realized what she said.

Damon laughed. "Thank you for being honest with me. What else?"

"Let's see. Mainly massage, a spanking horse without bondage, and general light play."

"What kind of implements on the spanking horse?"

"Hand, a paddle, and a light flogger."

"No crop or cane?" He noticed she'd specified 'maybe' rather than listing that as a hard or soft limit.

"I haven't tried them. I'm not sure I'd like them. I'm not into pain."

"I don't enjoy inflicting pain, only pleasure." He ran his fingers over her hair. "Tell me what you mean by light play."

Tessa closed her eyes as he caressed her hair. His touch was comforting. "Nudity and touching. Watching scenes together. That's really it outside of the massage or impact play."

"Sex?"

Her tummy tightened. "Damon, I didn't have a romantic relationship with my Dom. He was my mentor, nothing more." She took a deep breath. "We never had sex."

"So you kept your personal life and club life separate."

"I tried." And she'd tried hard until her idiot ex-fiancé. Why she ever thought Jack would enjoy a little spice in their love life was beyond her. At the time, she thought it would be nice. "I was foolish to think the two could mix together."

Damon frowned. "Our friends are making it work."

"Yes, but…" Her friends didn't have the background she did. If anyone unearthed who her father was and sold her out to the press… She shuddered.

"We can start with club play and see how things go. Can you do that?"

She nodded.

"Good." He fell silent.

Tessa laid there feeling a sense of peace flow over her. How long had it been since she'd relaxed and taken in life? A while. Her lashes drifted shut as Damon gently stroked her hair.

* * * *

Damon grinned when Tessa's breathing settled into a deep, contented pattern. She'd fallen asleep. He wasn't sure how he felt about keeping club life separate from everyday life, but he would do it for now. Especially since she didn't know what he did for a living.

He relaxed and began to plan out how Thursday night would go and the nights after that. He was going to have fun playing with Tessa. A romantic relationship would either come naturally or not at all. Though he hoped the former came true.

They weren't off to a bad start. She'd had dinner with him Friday night and the picnic today. And she'd been open and honest. Damon's grin widened. He was ready to deal with Tessa and whatever she threw at him.

CHAPTER SEVEN

Damon made his way to his workshop Monday morning, his mind still filled with Tessa. He'd taken her home yesterday, telling her he'd see her Thursday night, and gave her a kiss that left his dick begging for relief.

He flipped on the lights and shivered. He must have forgotten to leave the furnace turned up so the place would be warm. Once his equipment started running, it would get warm enough. Moving over to his work desk, he looked at what orders he had.

A couple of his specialized vibrators, nipple clamps, and one of his harnesses. He checked his supplies. He had everything. First, he'd work on the vibrators.

Making adult toys wasn't the plan when he went to MIT, but one summer, he was at loose ends and applied for a job with a film company, not knowing it was an adult film company. He learned a lot that summer about the industry but also heard complaints about toys, how they broke often, and sometimes the production needed something different.

He'd started playing with ideas on paper, then was able to find a place where he could experiment. It took him a while, but he began to improve the toys. Vibrators, for example. Some had one speed, others had multiple, but one of his biggest sellers was one that had not only multiple speeds, but also rotated.

How would Tessa take to his toys? There were a few people in the club who knew about his toy making, but most of his orders came over the internet. Sitting down at his workbench, Damon began to construct the first vibrator.

Maybe he'd take one to the club on Thursday and see how Tessa reacted.

His lips tilted up. Oh yes, and maybe it was time to experiment with some other things he was thinking of making. Tessa would be the best test subject...if she agreed.

* * * *

Tessa stared at her closet. What to wear tonight? Damon had texted her earlier, asking if she needed his help with an outfit, and she told him no. They'd exchanged numbers Sunday when he brought her home.

Let's see what I can find. Ten minutes later, she had a black skirt and her black flats, but top-wise, she was lost. She dug around and found a red lace cami that would work with the skirt. After finding a small bag, she put all the items into it.

Since the club had a nice place to change and secure lockers for personal items, she'd change there. She was glad for that. Her favorite raincoat was currently drying out since it was raining today. Better than snow, but it was going to make for a rough drive out to the club.

She'd planned on driving herself, but Damon vetoed the idea, telling her he didn't want her driving after they spent time in the club. Tessa wanted to argue with him, but she heard the firmness in his voice and decided they could discuss it as he drove tonight.

Now, the idea of a discussion about control while he drove in this weather might not be such a good idea. Tessa grabbed one of her hooded sweatshirts, pulled it on over her street clothes, then put her wallet and cell in the bag with her clothes. The doorbell rang, and she opened the door to Damon.

"Oh goodness." She jogged to the bathroom and came

back with a towel. Damon was soaked. "I take it the weather is still stormy."

"To say the least." Damon rubbed the towel over his face and hair.

"Get in here." Tessa pulled him into her apartment. "Why don't you go in the guest bathroom, get out of those wet clothes, and take a hot shower."

"Trying to get me out of my clothes." His eyes twinkled.

"Trying to keep you from catching a cold." She pushed him toward the bathroom. "I can put your clothes in the dryer while you're in the shower and find you something to put on while they dry."

"Or I could run around naked."

Tessa shook her head, and he laughed and made his way down the hall. Tessa dug around in the back of her closet for an old pair of her brother's sweats. They should fit. She heard the shower come on, then she opened the bathroom door an inch.

"Are you in the shower?"

"Yes. Planning to join me?"

"You wish." His teasing was becoming second nature. She set the sweats down and picked up his wet clothing. "Sweats on the counter."

After throwing his clothes in the washer, she looked out her balcony window. Yep, there was a storm all right, complete with wind. Tessa grabbed her cell and called the club. "Wicked Sanctuary, this is Max."

"Hey, Max, Tessa here."

"What's up, lovely lady?"

"I don't think Damon and I are going to make it with the storm that's brewing."

"There's a storm?" She could hear movement on the

other end before Max came back on the phone. "Holy crap. Stay home. I looked out. I had no idea."

"Yeah, I didn't either. Be safe and tell Sierra I'm fine."

"I'm sure you are." The line went dead.

Tessa looked at her phone. It flashed no service. That was odd. Then the lights flickered. Crap. She quickly opened her cabinets and got out her lanterns. A roll of thunder sounded, and the lights flickered again.

"Damon, you better hurry. We might lose power." Tessa opened the freezer and grabbed a jug of frozen water and stuck it in the fridge. She always kept a couple frozen—just in case.

The bathroom door opened as the lights went out. Tessa turned on one of the battery-powered lanterns.

"Sounds like the storm has intensified," he said, walking toward her with towels in his hands.

"Yeah. Drop those on the washer. It looks like it will be a while before you'll have dry clothes." She glanced over at him; the sweats were a little tight. Where her brother was skinny, Damon was muscled. "Sorry those don't fit better."

"They're okay, but I'm wondering why you have men's sweats. These would not fit you."

Tessa laughed. "They're my brother's. I accidently packed them when I moved here."

"He doesn't miss them?"

"No." Allen didn't have time to miss them. He was too busy trying to follow in his father's footsteps, so three-piece suits were more the norm. "I called Max and told him we wouldn't be at the club tonight."

Damon walked over to her balcony doors. "Is it okay if I open them?"

"Sure."

He opened one door, and the wind whipped into her apartment. Damon shut the door. "What a wind. The way it looks out there, I doubt anyone makes it to the club, not with this kind of storm."

"Not the night we had planned." Tessa wondered what they could do. If she was alone, she'd curl up in bed. She could do that with Damon. Her muscles froze. Too soon to think about them in bed together.

"No, but I have an idea." He moved her small table and chairs away from the balcony windows, then grabbed the cushions and pillows from the sofa and arranged them on the floor. "Now we can watch the storm."

A quiver slipped up Tessa's spine.

"What is it?"

Trust him to see something even though the only light they had was from the lantern. "I'm not very fond of storms." She jumped as thunder rolled.

"Come here." Damon pulled her to him. He took the lantern from her hand and placed it on the table before leading her over to the cushions. "Sit down." He helped her down to the floor, but stayed standing.

When she was seated, he slid behind her before lowering his body to the floor, his legs on either side of her body. He grabbed a cushion and put it behind his back before grabbing a pillow.

"Come on." With his hand on her shoulder, he urged her to lie back until her back met his chest. He placed the small pillow under her head.

"Better?" he asked. His arms looped around her waist, his hands resting on her abs.

"This is nice," she whispered. It was. His chest was warm even though he had no shirt on. Being held close to him helped her feel safe and secure.

Lightning flashed, and she flinched.

"Easy. I'm right here. It can't hurt you."

"Sorry." Tessa ducked her head.

"Hey." Warm fingers caressed her chin. "What made you afraid of storms?"

A tremor worked its way through her body. "It was a long time ago, but I've never been able to shake it."

"Do you want to talk about it?"

"It seems kind of silly."

"If it's still affecting you, it's not silly."

Tessa tilted her head so she could see his face. Sincerity was written there. He believed the words he said. She slouched against him. "I was about eight years old. We were out in the country, visiting my aunt. A storm came up."

"Was this back when you lived in DC?"

"Yep. Thunder and lightning, the whole nine yards. I'd been outside with my brother. I didn't care about getting wet. We were kids." She took a breath. "Anyway, lightning flashed, and a bolt came right down and hit a tree not far from where I was standing."

"It could have hit you." His voice was soft.

"Scared me to death. I started running and screaming. My brother laughed at me."

"If I ever meet him, remind me to punch him for that."

Tessa's lips turned up. "We were both quite young. Since then, storms bother me. My father told me to get over it; I wouldn't be hurt by a storm. But I couldn't shake what happened. I was born and raised in DC, but I'd never been outside during a bad storm."

His arms tightened around her. "We don't get storms like this too often, but we do have them. How did you get through them?"

"Most of the time, they're at night, so I can curl up in my bed or distract myself with the TV, but with the electricity out…"

"Well then, let me distract you." He lowered his head and captured her lips.

Tessa didn't hesitate. She opened her mouth to Damon's. His tongue swept in. She twisted within his hold so they were face to face. The feel of his hands stroking her back set her blood on fire.

Her hands wandered to his hair-roughened chest. So strong and manly. She shifted so she could stroke farther south.

"Tessa." Damon pulled his lips from hers.

"What? Can't I play?" Where were the words coming from? She usually wasn't this flirty or forward. It wasn't how she'd acted with her mentor. Hell, with *any* man.

"Maybe." He nuzzled her cheek then pulled back, putting some distance between them. "I don't want you to feel rushed or pressured. We can lie here all night together and watch the storm."

"Are you saying this is up to me?" This was different. She wasn't sure how she felt about that. Tessa expected him to take command.

"Yes."

"But what if you don't want to play?" She'd never been with a man so open, so willing to listen to her wants and needs. She refused to take advantage of him.

"Then I would tell you. This isn't a one way street." His finger brushed over her cheek. "I will be open and honest with you. I expect the same."

"This is very unexpected." How open and honest did she need to be with Damon? Yes, tonight they'd planned to go to the club but more as trainer and trainee. Nevertheless, her body was ready to play with him. Thunder rumbled, and she flinched.

"Relax." Damon tugged her down until she lay on his chest. "It's just the two of us. We don't have to do anything."

"But—" She bit her lip and sighed as she felt the tension and anxiety slowly drain from her body. He'd keep her safe, and she let her worries slip away.

* * * *

Damon grinned as Tessa relaxed against him. He wanted nothing more than to scoop her up into his arms and carry her into the bedroom, but he'd wait until she was ready.

She might say she was ready, but this was more than needing to scratch an itch for him, and he suspected it was that way for her as well. Her fingers made circles on his chest. His blood heated at her touch.

"Will you touch me?" she whispered, her breath caressing his skin.

An idea formed in his mind. "Let's do this. I want you to strip off your top and sit back between my legs like we were."

"Okay." Tessa rocked back onto her knees, stripped off her shirt, and reached for her bra.

"Leave the bra on," he ordered.

"Yes, Sir."

His dick stiffened at her words.

Tessa scooted around, sat between his legs, and leaned back.

Oh, yes. This was good. He had access to her breasts, and when she was ready, he'd slip his hands down her pants and find her pussy.

"Close your eyes," he said, his lips next to her ear. Her

lashes fluttered down. "I wanted to play with these beauties tonight at the club." He kept his tone low as his palms cupped her fabric-clad breasts. "I felt them pressing against my chest that night as we danced. So full and firm."

A small tremor shook her body as he brushed his thumbs over her hard nipples beneath the lace. Good, she reacted to his words and his voice. He didn't want her to zone out again, so he kept his tone low and even, avoiding the husky deep voice he used when in a scene.

Lightning flashed, and Tessa jumped.

"Easy, sweetie. The storm can't touch you here in my arms." He found the front clasp of her bra and flicked it open. She drew in a sharp breath and let it out.

"So beautiful." And they were. "Your skin is flushing, and your nipples are hard."

"Please," she whispered.

"Please what?" He circled her areola with his finger, not touching the nipple.

"Damon…Sir…please touch me."

He flicked her right hardened peak with his nail.

Her neck arched as she moaned.

Then he did the same to her left one. Another moan.

Damon lifted his hand to her chin and tilted her head back. He took her lips with his as he pinched her nipples.

Her cry of surprise was swallowed by his kiss, but she didn't pull away; instead, she pushed her breasts into his hands. Yes, they were going to have fun tonight.

* * * *

Tessa wondered if the storm outside had invaded her body. Her skin was alive with tingles spreading over her when Damon touched her. When he pinched her nipples, her stomach turned over with butterflies, and she cried out into his mouth, not in pain, but in surprise and pleasure.

She shifted between his legs as her pussy throbbed while he continued to kiss her and play with her breasts, his touch alternating from soft to rough. And her body ate it up. She hadn't expected all this heat sweeping through her. Not at all.

Her body had never responded like this to any man. Damon's touch called to her, caused her body to go up like a furnace, and she was going to answer. She wanted more from him. She tore her lips from his.

"More, Damon," she whispered.

"No topping from the bottom." He nipped at her lips.

She groaned. "Please…Sir." She needed more.

"Let's see." He rolled her nipples between his fingers.

"Oh yes, Sir."

Her tummy quivered as he slid his one hand down over her abs, then to the waistband of her jeans. Aw shit, she was still wearing her jeans and shoes. She wanted them off; she wanted to feel his skin against hers.

Damon cupped her mound. She moaned. "Let me get these jeans off," she whispered.

"No." His voice was firm.

Instantly, her breath caught in her throat at that voice. Damn, what was it about his voice that did that to her? She'd been around other men with deep husky tones like Damon, but there was underlying steel to his voice that instantly made her blood boil and her bones melt.

"Please, Sir. I want your touch."

"And you will have it."

She breathed a sigh of relief.

"When I'm ready to give it to you."

Shit. He pressed his fingers against the seam of her jeans where it covered her pussy. Unable to stop herself, she bent her knees and opened herself to him.

"Vixen." He nipped her ear as his fingers danced over her fabric-covered mound.

Tessa couldn't help herself; she shifted her groin. Damon removed his hand, and she moaned.

"We're going to do this my way," he declared.

"Yes, Sir." While she wanted more, he was right. She was trying to top from the bottom.

"Sit up." Tessa complied.

Damon stood up. "Stay here." He went into the kitchen. Tessa debated following him, but he'd told her to stay. She would show him she could follow his orders, make him proud of her.

He came back with something hidden behind his back. "Stand up."

Tessa swallowed and did as he asked. The sweat pants he wore outlined his hard cock. A bolt of excitement flowed through her veins, knowing she made him hard. She started to reach out and at the last second pulled her hand back.

"Please strip." His voice was husky, but gentle.

She rose to her feet, removed her bra, toed off her shoes, and pulled her jeans, panties, and socks off. Tessa straightened and met Damon's gaze. Her breath whooshed out of her at the heat in his eyes.

"Damn, woman." He placed something on the sofa where she couldn't see it, then he began rearranging the pillows, before holding his hands out to her. Without hesitation, she put her hands in his.

"I'm going to help you to the floor and arrange you the way I want you."

"Yes, Sir." Was that her breathless voice? Damon did that to her.

"Please kneel down."

She knelt, while he held her hands.

"Now, sit, then lie back."

Tessa took a deep breath. She was putting a lot of trust in Damon; then again, if she didn't trust him, she wouldn't have asked him to be her trainer.

Once she was on her ass, she leaned back, and Damon slowly lowered her to the floor.

"Easy," he said once she was lying on the floor. He knelt down and adjusted the pillow beneath her neck so it supported her head better. "Okay?"

"I'm fine, Sir."

He grinned and dropped a kiss on her nose before he moved to her legs. "I want you to lift your fine ass off the floor."

Heat flooded her face, but she did as he asked, and he slipped two pillows under her. One at the small of her back, the other beneath her ass. Her legs fell open naturally, the cool air in the room caressing her slit.

"Very nice," he said, rising to his feet. "Don't move. I'll be right back."

He disappeared. Tessa wondered what he was doing. The low rumble of thunder flowed through the room. Damon came back, holding a towel and one of her scarves.

"Are you okay with me using your scarf as a blindfold?"

"Yes, Sir." A thrill of anticipation skimmed over her skin. She'd only experienced a blindfold once with her mentor in DC. When he'd blindfolded her, he'd told her to use her other senses. He'd also told her that the blindfold would help her to learn to trust her Dom.

Damon knelt by her head and placed the scarf over her eyes. He gently lifted her head and tied it. She couldn't see anything. Then she giggled. The power was out; of course, she couldn't see much. The lantern gave off low light.

"Is that comfortable?"

"Yes, Sir."

"I want to hear you, so any noises you want to make, make them. Safe words?"

"Yellow to slow down. Red to stop."

"Right. Now let's have some fun."

Tessa turned her head, forgetting she couldn't see. So she closed her eyes and listened. Something clinked together and silence. Warm hands touched her knees, and she jumped.

"Just me, sweetie." There was a twinge of humor in his voice.

She blew out a breath and calmed her nerves. Damon's touch was soft as he skimmed his fingers from her knees up the inside of her thighs. Her muscles quivered as he pushed her thighs apart, exposing her further.

"So pretty," he whispered as he drew a finger over her slit.

It took everything she had not to squirm under his touch as her pussy clamped down.

Then he blew over her mound. She groaned as her muscles tightened with need. His cheek rubbed the inside of her left thigh as his fingers parted her slit. His hot breath caressed her skin.

"Ohhhhh!" The exclamation slipped from her lips when he ran his tongue over her slit and caressed her clit. Moisture gathered in her pussy.

"I need a better taste," he whispered.

Before she could reach, his mouth closed over her pussy. Thankfully, he'd put his hands on her hips, which prevented her from lifting up. "Fuck," she whispered as he ran his tongue through her folds, darting into her pussy and back out to tease her clit.

98

Her toes curled into the light carpeting. One swipe of his tongue and her body was on fire.

"Very sweet," he remarked after raising his head. "You're all flushed, sweetie. Are you enjoying this?"

"Yes, Sir." She forced the words past her lips, her choppy breath not leaving much room for words.

"Good. Let's see if I can make you fly."

Before she could think of what his words meant, his mouth closed over her clit, and he thrust a finger into her pussy.

This time, she arched her hips. *Oh my goodness.* His finger twisting in her pussy, along with his tongue playing with her clit and teasing it, made her muscles clench.

Damon withdrew his finger, and Tessa drew in several sharp breaths only to lose it again as he thrust in two fingers.

"How long has it been for you?" he asked, lifting his head and wiggling his fingers.

He asked her a question? Oh yes. "Several years." He was a sorcerer. No man had got her this hot and bothered so quickly.

"Poor Tessa."

Her only warning was the puff of his breath before he captured her clit once again.

Her head twisted on the pillow. Without thought, she raised her hands to find his head. Her fingers brushed his hair, and he stopped moving his fingers and lifted his head.

"Hands down."

With his order, she dropped her arms to her sides and felt her body sink against the carpet.

"No touching."

"But—"

"No buts. Keep your hands at your sides, or I'll stop."

Damn Dom. After a few moments, he started again.

Her body hadn't even had time to cool off. Each flick of his tongue against her clit and thrust of his fingers took her higher and higher. A bolt of lightning shot from her clit to her nipples and back again.

She wasn't going to last long. Quivers ran through her muscles, causing her toes and fingers to curl into the carpet. As if Damon knew what was going on, he began to thrust his fingers harder and faster.

Tessa opened her mouth but found she could barely breathe, so words weren't going to happen, no matter what she wanted to say to him.

Damon curled his fingers, and Tessa cried out as her climax rolled over her. The tremors shook her body. But Damon didn't stop; his tongue kept tormenting her clit. She twisted her head as she heard something. A clink or a clank of something he was picking up. What devious plan did this man have now?

Barely as the thought formed, she cried out again.

Ice. He'd put *ice* on her nipple. The sensation carried her to orgasm again. "Damon," she whispered. She couldn't take it. Her senses were on overload.

"Easy, sweet Tessa." The ice moved to the other nipple, and while she didn't cry out this time, a moan left her lips.

"Too much." She fought to get the words out. Then the world faded out.

* * * *

Tessa's body went lax, and Damon dropped the ice cube. "Tessa?" He drew off the scarf. Her eyes were closed, and her breathing labored. Damon checked her pulse, rapid but steady.

Should he call 911? Then she moaned. "Tessa." Damn

100

it, he'd rather cut off his right arm than see her hurt. "Sweetie." He put his arms around her and held her in a sitting position, supporting her head.

"You killed me," she whispered.

"What?" Her pulse was steady.

"You killed me with pleasure." Her lashes rose.

"Sweetheart, are you okay?"

Her brown eyes were languid, and a smile played around her lips. "I'm fine. Kind of passed out from all that bliss."

"Don't scare me like that." Damon rose to his knees, then lifted her into his arms.

"Damon?" Her arms went around his neck.

"Shhhh." He was glad he'd put one of the lanterns in the bedroom earlier. He carried her into the room and laid her on the bed. "Stay put."

Damon quickly turned off the lantern in the other room and put the glass of ice in the kitchen before returning to the bedroom with a glass of water for Tessa.

Tessa was on her side, her eyes half open. "Devious man," she whispered.

He grinned. "Drink." He helped her sit so she could drink. She was okay. The tightness in his chest lessened. She finished the water, and he put the glass on the nightstand, climbed onto the mattress, and pulled her into his arms. His cock pulsed with need, but he ignored it the best he could. This was about her.

"I can't believe I passed out." Her voice was getting stronger.

"The last thing you said was too much." He tightened his arms around her as his fear of losing her receded.

"The sensations. I'm having a hard time describing them."

"Was it the ice?" He'd played with ice before but never with her reaction.

"Ice, heat, everything. It was like I was in pleasure overload. That's the only way I can explain it."

"I'll remember that." His lips brushed her forehead. "Rest." He reached over and turned the lantern off. Tessa snuggled against him. It took Damon some time to fall asleep. She was safe in his arms. He knew that, but her reaction had scared the crap out of him. He couldn't lose her. He wouldn't.

CHAPTER EIGHT

The next morning, Tessa sat at the table while Damon cooked. "You never did tell me what you do with your engineering degree." She'd offered to help him, but he told her to sit down and let him surprise her.

"I'm not sure you're ready for that yet."

"Come on, Damon. We slept together last night." With the storm last night, power was still out in places, and trees were down on roadways. Though her power had come back on, her boss had texted her that, since there was no power at the library, she should stay home.

He stayed silent as he slid two perfect omelets onto plates and carried them to her small table. Damon set her plate in front of her and turned his head. "I need to hear specific consent that you want to know what I do with my degree."

Her eyes widened. "Don't you think we're past the consent phase?"

"Not for this." He stared at her. "I've had some bad reactions to what I do for a living."

"I want to hear." He grinned before taking his seat and setting his food down. "What could be so private you needed consent from me?" She picked up her coffee mug and took a sip.

"Because I use my engineering degrees to make adult toys."

Tessa almost spit out the coffee in her mouth. Instead, she started coughing. Damon rose, but she waved him back down. She had tears in her eyes by the time she got her coughing fit under control.

"Not what I was expecting to hear." She took a small sip of water and caught her breath.

"Now you know why I needed consent."

"How did you get into designing adult toys? Somehow, I don't think there are college classes for that." She took a bite of her ham, cheese, and spinach omelet. It melted in her mouth. This man could cook.

"By accident. I was an electrical engineering student, and one summer I took a summer job, not realizing it was on an adult film crew."

Tessa stared at him. "How did you not know?"

"They advertised for an electrician to help with lighting. I thought it was a wiring job."

"Must have been a surprise when you found out what the job really was." She finished her omelet.

"It was, but since I was already in the lifestyle, I decided, why not?"

"So what were you doing?"

"Actually helping with the lighting. Making sure the lights were in working order and holding them when needed."

"How did that evolve into making adult toys?"

"They were using dildos and vibrators on the set, and the female leads kept complaining how unrealistic they were. It got me thinking. So I started designing some toys. Even when college classes started back up, I'd go visit the film company and talk with everyone about the toys."

"You had a built-in test group."

He laughed. "I guess I did. I've never thought of it that way." He finished his food and took a drink of his coffee. "You're taking this very well."

"Why wouldn't I? It's fascinating." She rested her chin

in her hand. "Have people reacted badly?"

"Not people in the lifestyle, but outside of it, yes."

"They don't understand?"

"There is that. My ex-girlfriend thought I could do better in life than make adult toys."

"Based on what I saw of your home, I'd say you're doing pretty darn well."

"I have a good clientele."

"Does that include the adult film industry?"

"It does." He flashed her a smile. "What started off as a small thing turned into a big business for me."

"I love it." She stood and picked up their plates. "I think it's fantastic you can do something you love, and it makes you money."

"What about you?" He followed her with their empty coffee mugs. "Do you love being a librarian?"

"Actually, I do." She did love her job. "My job is good to me, and I'm lucky enough to make a good salary."

"I hear a but in there."

"Yes and no. When I was in high school, I really wanted to work in a museum."

"The Smithsonian."

"Yep. There's so much history in DC. I wanted to explore it all."

"I hear the passion in your voice. Why didn't you pursue history and find your niche? I can't see you being afraid of hard work."

"It wasn't that." She pushed away from the sink. "My father is in politics, and that makes life a little more difficult."

"You mentioned your father didn't approve of you going into library science."

"He didn't. He also didn't want me getting a degree in

art or archeology or museum studies either. I really wanted to be a curator, so that meant master's degree, the work experience, and possibly a PhD. After all that, library science was a better option.

Damon rubbed his forehead. "I don't see what the issue was. You don't strike me as someone who gives up that easily. Especially for a career you clearly wanted to have."

"You have to think about politics. Perception is everything and so is appearance. While working for a museum is an honorable job, those jobs were for other people, not me. My father wanted me to find a young man who had political aspirations and become the best political wife in the world."

"Tessa, you're a great woman, but I can't see you holding your tongue with some of these, shall we say, not too bright politicians. Including your father."

She snorted. "You have that right. At one party, someone was talking—I can't even remember about what—and they had the facts all wrong. I gently corrected him, and I got this, 'Oh honey, you're so cute. Now go run along.' I lost it. Let me tell you, no one was a happy camper after the party. Especially my father."

"I would've loved to see you let them have it." He guided her to her sofa. "So, since you have the day off, what shall we do?" His fingers played with her hair.

"Don't you have work to do?"

"I'm fine. I do need to run over to Colby's shop to see if he can make us some new wristbands."

"Colby? "

"Yeah, he runs Durham's Leather Shop."

"Oh, that new place that opened down the street from Lara's cafe."

"That's it."

"Okay. News reports say most of the damage and power outages are on the way out of town, not in town. Except for the library. There's a big tree in the parking lot. Go do what you need to do, and we can have dinner tonight in town."

"Why don't you come with me? We can have lunch at Sweet and Savory, grocery shop, and I'll cook you dinner at my place. They should have the roads cleaned up by then."

"But you already cooked me breakfast."

"If you haven't already noticed, I like cooking. And you, my lady, loved every bite of that omelet." He paused. "Please."

Tessa chuckled. "There you go with those big eyes and fluttering lashes. Okay, let me get dressed. Your clothes are dry, I made sure to get them washed and dried this morning."

"What? You don't like me in the sweats?" He stood up, and the fabric outlined his hard cock.

She closed her eyes so as not to reach out and cup him. "Behave, Damon."

"That's no fun." He pulled her up from the sofa. "Go dress, and if you're really good, I'll buy you dessert after lunch."

"I'll be a perfect angel." She shimmied into the bedroom and closed the door, laughing. There was something about Damon that brought out her wild side.

* * * *

A rich, earthy smell greeted Tessa as she walked into Durham's Leather Shop with Damon. She'd been a little uneasy when she saw all the motorcycles parked outside. She'd never been around bikers.

Damon kept his arm around her waist as he guided her to a man with short black hair, his navy T-shirt clinging to his chest and outlining his broad shoulders. "Hey, Colby."

"Hey, Damon." The man held his hand out.

Tessa glanced around the shop as they shook hands. Biker guys mingled around the shop. Some of the bikers were big guys with tattoos and in leather, whereas others were kind of normal looking guys in jeans and boots. Her gaze took in the rows and rows of amazing leather goods. There was a portioned off section with a sign that said 'Over 21 Only.' She was intrigued.

"Tessa, this is Colby."

"Hello."

"Hi, Tessa." He smiled. "Are you looking for something special?"

"Actually, I was hoping you had a few minutes to chat," Damon said. "Max, Jordan, and I talked about something different for the wristbands and were wondering if you could make something for us."

"Sure. Let's go sit down." He gestured to an area with a couple of leather-covered chairs and a sofa.

"Great." Damon looked down at her. "Do you want to explore or sit with us?"

"I want to sit with you. I'm curious what you're going to have Colby do."

"You know, curiosity can kill," Damon whispered with laughter in his voice as he guided her to the sofa.

"Very funny."

Damon sat down next to her, his thigh touching hers. Colby took the chair across from them.

"So what are you guys thinking about?" Colby asked.

"We've been having issues lately with the wristbands catching on stuff. When we first started using them, it wasn't an issue. But now it seems they're starting to fray and catch on equipment."

"That can be a problem."

"So we were thinking if you could do some sort of leather type band that we could use. Something that wouldn't interfere with play but also with restraints or anything like that."

"I'm pretty sure I can. But silicone would be a better choice for cleaning purposes. The only problem might be the fastener. I can't use anything too big."

"Can you make them in colors?"

"Oh yeah, that's right, the bands are color coded." Colby rubbed his chin. "That shouldn't be a problem. Here's the forty-thousand-dollar question. How soon do you want them?"

"Can you do some mock-ups so we can see what you can come up with? We're willing to pay you for them."

Colby waved his hand. "No need. I can do mock-ups. Say, in a few weeks I'll have some ready for you?"

"That's great. Thanks."

"Sure." The men stood and shook hands, then Damon helped her to her feet.

"Would you like to look around?" Damon asked.

"I've been dying to." She was curious.

"Then let's go." Damon slipped his arm around her waist.

"You like touching me, don't you?" Not that she minded. She enjoyed his touch.

He grinned. "You have no idea, but this way, I can make sure you don't run away."

"I haven't run yet, have I?"

"No, but you never know."

Tessa didn't realize how big the shop was. While there were rows of jackets, vests, and chaps, there were also belts, bags, gloves, knife sheaths, and wallets. Damon guided her to the partitioned section.

"Oh my," she whispered when they entered. While the room wasn't huge, it was good sized. On the wall hung floggers, whips, and fetwear.

"Colby takes special orders," Damon said as he pulled a flogger off the wall. He twirled it, and she turned. His eyes narrowed. "Did you think I'd hit you?" He held the flogger out.

"No." She ran her fingers through the falls of the leather flogger. "I wasn't expecting it." Tessa put her hand on his tense forearm. "I know you would never hit me unless it was a negotiated scene."

His muscles relaxed under her fingers. She wondered why he'd tensed up so badly. Maybe something in his past. They had talked, but she was sure there were things neither of them had mentioned.

"Does Colby do a lot of custom work?" she asked as they left the adult stuff behind.

"He takes some. I know he has a small shop in the back of his store where he does his custom work."

"He's truly talented."

"Hey, Damon, come over here for a second," Colby yelled.

"Be right back."

Tessa started flipping through the leather bags. There were saddlebags, big leather bags, and some small ones. Nothing really for a woman. She moved toward the gloves.

"Can I help you with anything?" a male voice said next to her.

She looked up to see a young man with a buzz haircut, flashing green eyes, and a wide smile.

"I'm just looking."

"For anything special?"

"Not really."

"I'm Kase. If you need help with anything, please let me know. We only get a few of the bikers' women in here."

Tessa wondered why. "Do you have leather jackets for women?" Not that she planned on buying one, but she was curious.

"A few. Let me show you." Kase led her over to the small rack. There were maybe ten jackets on it.

"Thank you." She slid through the jackets on the rack. All small sizes and not much variation. She'd bet the men's weren't like this.

"Hey, Kase," a customer yelled.

"Be right there." Kase glanced down at her. "Holler if you need me." He loped off.

Tessa looked up to see Damon and Colby watching her, so she made her way to where the two men stood.

"Find anything you like?" Damon asked, his eyes twinkling with mischief.

"Not really." She looked at Colby. "You don't have a lot for women."

"I don't." Colby ran his hand over his short-cropped hair. "I've been trying to find a way to make the shop appeal to women. Not even my biker guys bring their old ladies here."

"Maybe because there's nothing for them." Tessa almost groaned. There went her mouth again.

Colby stared at her. "Any ideas? I'm open to them."

She bit her lip. Maybe he wouldn't take her words the wrong way. "There are no leather purses for women, so that would be a start. As for jackets, you have exactly ten, all in small sizes. As much as we women want to be skinny, we're not all a size two."

"What else?"

When she hesitated, he said. "Please, I really want to know."

"You do custom work, right?"

"I do."

"Advertise it. Women sometimes want something special for their man, even if they're not a biker. A wallet, belts, gloves, and probably even a jacket. I don't know what else you can make."

"I can do a lot of things." Colby stared down at her, a thoughtful look on his face.

"As for women's jackets, I would say if you are worried about inventory, keep one in each size and, if someone wants one, order it. If it happens to be a tourist, offer free shipping or something like that."

"Damn, why didn't I think of that?" Colby glanced at Damon. "Where did you find her?"

"My secret." Damon cradled her to his side.

"I'm the head librarian and have some contacts if you need to talk with other merchants."

"I might do that. Thank you for your input."

"Anytime."

Damon escorted Tessa out of the shop. "I think you made a friend," he said.

"Sometimes it just takes one person's input to see all the possibilities," she said as they walked hand in hand down the sidewalk to Lara's cafe.

* * * *

Saturday night the next week, Tessa pulled on a short black skirt and wiggled her way into a purple and black corset. She had several corsets in her closet. It felt good to wear one, but she'd forgotten how tight they could be. She loved hers because she could tighten them in the front, so no need for someone to help her.

Damon had brought her to his house, after a quick stop at hers so she could pack up an outfit for tonight. They'd had a nice dinner and, now, were both dressing for the club.

Tessa smiled. Damon told her they would play a little bit tonight. It didn't have to be a full-on scene, but he planned on touching her in the club. She didn't have a problem with that.

Who was she kidding? He'd already brought her to climax more than once with his touch. After the storm last week, they'd made it out to his house Friday afternoon. His property was undamaged. Lucky for him, trees had fallen in such a way that the driveway wasn't blocked.

He'd made her dinner and drove her home. He'd wanted to spend more time with her over the weekend, but the library opened Saturday morning, so she went in to help out, and on Sunday, she had things to do around her house. They'd gone to the club Thursday night for her class.

She stared at the two pairs of shoes she'd brought with her. Both black, one with three-inch spiked heels, the other one-inch wedges. She knew the club rules, so the wedges were out, but she also really didn't want to wear spiked heels. Darn it.

"Are you almost ready?" Damon yelled.

"Just a second." What was she going to do about shoes? She could go barefoot, but that didn't appeal either. She left the room carrying her shoes.

Damon looked up, and his eyes sparkled. "I like the outfit." His gaze roamed from her head to her toes. "Why are you holding your shoes?"

"I'm not very fond of spiked heels when I'm going to be on my feet all night, and I only brought a pair of wedges."

"Yeah, no wedges. You can go barefoot."

Tessa shook her head. "I don't like the idea of someone being able to step on my toes."

"If they do, I'll have their head. Haven't you noticed how many go barefoot?"

"Not really." Tessa tossed her shoes in the bag with her regular clothes. "There is a solution." She dug her phone out of her purse and dialed. "Hey, Sierra, can I borrow a pair of shoes for tonight? Yes, those will work. Thanks." Tessa smiled at Damon. "Problem solved."

"Good to have friends."

"I'm very fortunate to have them. Especially when they wear the same shoe size as me."

"Let's go."

Because they were at his house, it only took them about fifteen minutes to drive to the club. Damon turned down the road, stopped at the gate, and punched in the code, and waited.

"Not again," he said and punched in the code again. Nothing.

"You want me to call the club?"

"Not yet." He punched the code one more time. The gates swung open. "About time," Damon muttered. He drove through and waited to make sure the gates closed behind him. "I'll have to tell Max. I almost feel sorry for the gate company."

"Have you guys been having trouble with it?"

"We did. And the last time they were here Max told them to fix it or replace it. We thought it was fixed. It's almost like the gate has a mind of its own." He pulled into a parking spot and helped Tessa from the car.

She wobbled a bit in her heels and held tightly onto Damon's arm.

"I think I understand now why you didn't want to wear

them," he said as they made their way inside.

"Yeah, I used to be able to wear them often, but now my balance isn't what it used to be since I haven't worn them in some time."

Ralph was sitting at the table. "Evening, Master Damon, Ms. Tessa." He turned the sign in book around. They both signed, and Ralph handed Damon a purple and white wristband.

Damon slipped it on her right wrist, before he bent down. "Hand on my shoulder; I'm going to remove these shoes so you don't kill yourself."

Tessa did as he said and sighed as he removed her shoes. "I was crazy to think about wearing them, even for this short period of time."

Damon straightened and held the shoes out to her. "Go put them in a locker with your purse. I'm sure Sierra is waiting for you."

"Yes, Sir." She smiled and wiggled her hips as she walked down the hall.

"I'm so glad you're here." Sierra rushed over and hugged Tessa the second she stepped into the ladies' locker room.

"Me too." Tessa walked over to the lockers and put her stuff inside before shutting it.

"Here's the shoes." Sierra held out a pair of black satin slippers to her.

"Thank you. I can see I need to upgrade my shoes." Tessa sat down and slipped them on.

Sierra stared at her. "I've never seen that corset or skirt before."

Tessa's face grew warm. "Ummm, yeah. It was in the back of my closet."

"Are you going to be okay tonight?"

"Why shouldn't I?" Was there something she didn't know?

"I'm here, Crystal and Jordan should be here soon. We might all play later tonight." Sierra's cheeks turned pink.

"It's okay." Tessa stood up and smiled at her friend. "I don't know how much Damon and I will play tonight, but I can handle it."

"I'll admit we don't usually watch each other scene, but I have a feeling that the guys might team up at some point."

Tessa shivered thinking about their intense Doms.

"I bet they will." They walked out together to see Max and Damon talking.

The impact of Damon's gaze hit her like a freight train. Why now, she wasn't sure. Her nerves tingled with excitement.

"Our two beautiful women," Max said, coming over to them. He glanced at Damon who nodded. Max took Tessa's hands in his. "Welcome back. I'm glad you're here." He leaned down and kissed her cheek.

"Thank you, Max," Tessa said as he released her hands.

"What was that all about?" Sierra asked, her gaze going from Max to Damon and back.

"Protocol," Tessa said. "Max looked at Damon for permission to touch me." The familiar world of the lifestyle slid over her skin, and her muscles relaxed. Here she didn't have to make all the decisions. She could let Damon take control with the knowledge she was safe with him.

"Jordan said he will be here about ten." As Max pulled Sierra into his arms, Tessa smiled in silent reply to Sierra's knowing grin.

"I'll cover until he gets here," Damon said.

"Fine. We guys need to discuss how we want to go

about getting more help."

"Yep." Damon took her hand, and they made their way into the club. "I'm going to leave you in the green area for a bit while I work."

"Sure." He'd warned her this could happen. Damon was part-owner and worked the floor as well. The music was soft tonight, but she knew that would change later. It was early, barely after eight.

Damon escorted her to the green area where some of the club subs waited, then with a kiss, he sauntered away.

"Hi, Tessa," a female voice said.

Tessa turned her head. "Mistress Sage, how very nice to see you again." She'd helped Sage's sub, Brady during the court case when Jordan and Crystal had defended Sage.

"So those still waters really do hide secrets." Sage looked up and down.

Tessa's face flushed. "In a way. It's a long explanation."

"I have time. Brady won't be here for a bit. Let's sit down and you can tell me all about it." Sage gestured to an empty sofa. Tessa padded over and sat. This was going to be a different experience.

* * * *

Damon walked around the club, taking in all the scenes going on. Listening and watching. Not that they'd had any trouble, but it was part of his job. Every so often he'd look over to the green area. He was surprised to see Sage talking with Tessa. He shouldn't have been.

Sage was known to befriend subs and help them navigate the club protocols. But this seemed different, as if Tessa and Sage had met before. "Austin, that rope looks a little too tight," Damon said quietly.

"Damn," the Dom muttered. "I can't seem to get it

right."

"May I?"

"Please."

Damon stepped up onto the small stage and approached Austin and his sub. "May I touch her to show you how to get the rope tight without hurting her?"

"Yes, Master Damon."

"Roni, I'm going to touch your arm and wrist," Damon said. He liked to warn a sub when he was working with another Dom.

"Yes, Sir." Her voice was a bit shaky.

Damon released the rope, noting the red marks around her wrist. "Austin, her wrists are friction burned. You need to stop the scene and take care of her."

Austin swore when he saw his sub's wrists. "Honey, why didn't you say anything?" He knelt down in front of Roni so he could look in her face.

"I didn't want to stop the scene, Sir." Her voice wobbled.

"If you're hurting, even the tiniest bit, I want to know."

"Yes, Sir. I'm sorry."

"It's okay, my love, but we're going to discuss this." Austin rose to his feet. "Thank you for letting me know, Master Damon."

"You're welcome." Damon brushed his hand over Roni's head before standing. "I'll have one of the club subs bring you the first aid kit and some cold cloths to wrap around her wrists. They don't look bad but should be treated."

"Thank you again, Master Damon." Austin began undoing the rope around Roni's middle and her legs. Those had been done correctly.

"Austin, I'll talk with Master Max about having a

bondage class. I think some of the Doms could benefit from it."

"That would be helpful."

Damon stepped off the stage and spied Max a few stations down. He leisurely made his way toward Max, keeping an eye out as he walked. He stopped in his tracks when he saw a Dom approach Tessa.

Even from this distance, he could see Tessa stiffen, shake her head, and hold up her wrist. The Dom nodded, then backed away. Damon released the breath he didn't realize he'd been holding. Even with Sage sitting there, it still bothered him that the man had approached.

"He backed right off," Max said.

"I know."

"Then get that murderous look off your face before you scare everyone."

Damon took a breath. "I didn't realize I had a murderous look." Tessa was talking with Sage once again, her face glowing.

"Is everything okay with Austin and his sub?" Max asked.

"Yes. Friction burns from the rope." Damon shook his head. "Listen, would you be willing to teach a bondage class? I'm thinking some of the newer players could benefit."

"Not a bad idea. I've been thinking about how we might be able to expand our education classes."

Damon groaned. "More work for us."

"You're not one to shy away from more work. Are you available for a business meeting tomorrow?"

"I don't see why not, but I figured you'd be spending time with the lovely Sierra. In fact, where is she?"

"She went to help one of the subs in the ladies' room.

And usually, yes, Sundays are for Sierra and me, but she's having a girls' get-together."

"Tessa didn't mention it." He wondered why. "If they're getting together, then we can do our meeting at the same time."

"I believe they're getting together at Sierra's old apartment."

"I thought you'd convinced her to give it up and move in with you."

"I did, but the rent was paid through the end of the month, so she wanted to have one last girls' get-together there, before they have to figure out a new spot."

"Your house has room."

"Sierra wants it to be just the girls, no men. And no place where the men can overhear what the women are saying."

Damon rubbed his chin. "Sounds reasonable."

"I can't say I blame them. We all need to let off steam at one time or another."

"Yeah." Damon's mind went over something he'd read about Dom and sub groups. He needed to find that article again. Maybe this was something they could add to the growing list of things they wanted to do at the club.

Squeals of female voices floated through the club. Max and Damon looked to the green area. Crystal and Tessa were hugging, then Crystal hugged Sage, and Sierra jogged over to all of them.

"Damn, that's a beautiful sight," Jordan said, joining them.

"It is," Max said.

Damon nodded. He had to agree, seeing the four women was a sight to behold.

"Thanks for covering for me." Jordan clapped him on

the back.

"No problem."

"Jordan, Masters meeting tomorrow since the girls are going to be together," Max said.

"Works for me." Jordan adjusted his wristband.

"That reminds me," Damon said. "I talked with Colby. He's positive he can make something for us. He said he should have some mock-ups in a few weeks."

"Great," Max said. "We've had two incidents tonight with the bands. One snapped and went flying; the other got caught in the bondage system somehow, and we had to cut it off."

"Something more durable and less likely to snag will be great," Jordan said. "Now I'll take my turn as DM for a while."

"I'll be around if you need help," Damon said.

"So will I," Max echoed.

Jordan strolled off, and Max and Damon went to the green area. The women looked up as they arrived.

"Ladies." Max inclined his head.

"Sir," they all said.

"Master Max," Sage said.

"Let's go, love. I want to see if we can get a little bondage fun in tonight." Max took Sierra's hand, and off they went.

"No Brady tonight?" Damon asked Sage.

"He'll be here soon. He had an emergency at his job. But it worked out; I got to learn more about Tessa."

"It looked like you two already knew each other." Damon glanced from Sage to Tessa.

"In a way." Tessa glanced at Crystal.

"The case is over, so you can talk," Crystal said.

"How were you involved with Sage's case?" Damon

121

was well aware of the case, but didn't know Tessa had been involved.

"I wasn't really involved. I allowed Brady to stay at my apartment for a few days." Tessa looked down at her feet.

"She was a godsend," Sage said. "She provided a safe place for Brady."

"It was really nothing." Tessa's voice was quiet.

Damon sensed she was uncomfortable with the praise and wondered why. "Well, if you two will excuse us. I would like Tessa to watch some scenes tonight." He cupped her elbow and led her out of the green area.

"Damon, are you angry?" she asked as they walked.

"No. Why?" He glanced down at her and realized she was taking twice the number of steps he was. "Sorry. I didn't realize I was walking so fast."

"I thought maybe you were mad because I was talking with Sage."

"Of course not." He realized he hadn't gone over protocols with Tessa. While she was in the lifestyle, each club had their own protocols. Some were the same in every club, but it was always wise to review them. "My fault," he said, drawing her off to the side away from the people walking.

"Sir?" Her voice was soft as he pressed her up against the wall.

"I forgot to go over our protocols." He drew his finger over her cheek, enjoying the way her eyes grew soft at his touch. "Sir or Master in the club or bedroom. Talking to other subs is fine. Talking to anyone in the green area is fine as it's usually subs or Mistress Sage." He shifted his body closer. "Doms should respect the wristband, but you always have the final word. No is always acceptable. Even to me."

Her eyes widened. "I can say no to you in the club?"

"Yes. Just because I'm your Dom doesn't mean you're a doormat." He slipped his hand behind her neck. "I mean that, Tessa. I don't expect you to say yes to me because you think I expect it. I want you to say yes because you want it. Standard club safe words apply."

She tilted her head a tiny bit and stared at him. "Yes, Sir."

The way she said Sir made his cock harden to the point of pain. If this continued, he'd need to find different pants to wear. Right now, anyone could see how aroused he was.

"Little Tessa." He leaned down. "Do you have any idea what you do to me?"

"Probably the same thing you do to me, Sir." Her hands came up to his shoulders.

"Oh?" His fingers shifted on her neck to tangle in her hair. Her body sagged against his. "So I see. That is a very interesting trigger." He braced his body against hers.

"I don't know what it is, Sir," she whispered. "Having your hand in my hair with a little bit of pressure makes my knees turn to jelly. That only happens with you."

"Good to know." He released her hair. "I'd like you to watch a couple of scenes with me."

"I'd like that too, Sir." Her breathing was a little choppy.

Damon slipped his hands to her waist. "I know we talked, and you were okay with nudity in the club."

"I am, but not tonight, please, Sir."

"Not tonight. I like how you're dressed too much. I was thinking of others. The scenes I'd like us to observe will have partial to full nudity."

"I'll be fine, Sir."

"I hope so." Her breathing was normal, so Damon

123

stepped away from her. "Let's go." He kept his hand around her waist as they approached the first scene.

"Oh crap," she muttered.

"Do we need to go?" He'd deliberately picked Max and Sierra's bondage scene. If they were all going to play in the club together, she would have to get used to seeing her friends like this.

She shook her head. "I'll deal, Sir."

Pride in her swelled inside Damon. She was willing to try. He found an empty seat, so he sat down and pulled her into his lap.

* * * *

Tessa bit her lower lip so she didn't make a sound. This was all so unexpected. Yes, she knew she'd eventually see her friends playing in the club. But not what was essentially her fourth visit.

She glanced up at the stage. Oh my. Sierra was in a bondage chair, and Max was doing some intricate bondage around her breasts. Tessa swallowed.

"Is this too much for you?" Damon whispered against her ear.

"No, Sir. Those ties are quite intricate." She watched as Max wound the rope around, making Sierra's breasts more prominent, but not cutting into her skin. Sierra's expression was calm.

Max stopped and talked to her. She smiled and replied. Max continued down her torso. "It's not Shibari, is it, Sir?" It didn't look like it to her.

"Yes and no. Max doesn't do the really intricate Shibari, but he enjoys rope play and is very good at it."

"So I see, Sir." Max stopped frequently to check in with Sierra.

"Notice how intimate he is with her. Not only talking,

but the way his fingers skim over her skin as he wraps the rope around her."

"Making sure it isn't too tight, Sir?"

"Correct." His arms tightened around her waist. "Max is super careful because Sierra's skin is soft, and he doesn't want to harm her."

"I would think no Dom wants to harm their sub, Sir." Tessa shivered. She'd seen a sadist once at a DC club. She'd run out of the room, but the images still stayed with her.

"What is that shiver about?" Damon lifted his hand and caressed her cheek.

"I'm sorry, Sir. I don't understand sadists or masochists either. But my kink isn't their kink and as long as it's consensual, to each their own."

"The pain that sadist inflict on a masochists is not harm in the widely understood sense of the word. The pain is satisfying to both. We may not understand other's needs, but it's theirs and theirs alone. That's why the lifestyle is freeing. We're able to express our sensuality and sexuality anyway we want."

A soft cry came from the stage, and Tessa's attention was pulled back to Max and Sierra. Max was now lightly swatting Sierra's breasts with a rabbit flogger. Tessa's nipples tightened in response.

"Red! Fuck it! Red." The yell came from across the room. Max looked over with a frown on his face.

"Be right back, sweetie." Damon stood and placed her in the chair. "Stay there, do not move." Then he left.

Tessa was tempted to stand up to see what was going on, but Damon had told her not to, and she was going to obey, even if her curiosity was aroused.

Max was still staring across the room, then his features

lightened. "All is well, folks," he said to the audience watching him and Sierra. But the mood was broken, Sierra was talking to Max and shaking her head. Crystal stood nearby.

The crowd started to disperse. Tessa turned in her chair in the direction Max had been looking. She saw Harper, one of the club subs, shaking her head and gesturing with her hands. Jordan was standing with another man. His face was red, and he was obviously angry.

"I did not agree to that." Harper's words carried across the room. It was then Tessa saw she was crying. Orders or no orders. Harper needed another sub to comfort her.

Before she realized she'd moved, Tessa was out of the chair and across the room. Damon frowned at her when she came up to Harper and put her arm around the woman's shoulders. "It will be okay," Tessa whispered.

Harper leaned against her. Tessa spoke to Damon. "Sir, I'm going to take her over to the aftercare area."

He nodded, and Tessa led Harper over to a sofa and sat down beside her. "I'm here for you, Harper."

"I don't understand," Harper said sniffling.

"Here." Crystal thrust tissues into Harper's hands. "Tell us what happened?"

"I've played with Peter before." Harper wiped away her tears. "We've always been compatible."

"What changed tonight?" Tessa kept her arm around Harper's shoulders, giving her a light squeeze.

"I don't know. We discussed the scene, and then—wham—he wanted to change it. He wanted to use the bullwhip on me." A shudder shook her frame.

"Is the bullwhip a hard limit?" Crystal asked.

"Yes. It's one thing I do refuse. Yes, I like pain but not that kind of pain." Another tremor racked Harper's body. "I tried it once, and I had bruises for a week and several small cuts that healed, thankfully."

Crystal's eyes narrowed. "Okay. You stay here with Tessa. I'm going to go talk with Jordan."

"Crystal…" Tessa didn't want her friend to get into trouble, but she was already moving away.

"Thank you for being so kind. Not that Master Damon wasn't, but…" Her voice trailed off.

"But he's a man." Tessa finished for her. "I understand." Sometimes a woman needs another woman, or in this case another sub, to fully understand the issues. "Close your eyes and relax." Tessa lowered her arm as Harper scooted down and rested her head against the back of the sofa.

Tessa suddenly realized the club was quiet. She glanced around the room. It was empty except for Max, Jordan, Damon, Sierra, Crystal, Peter, Harper, and herself. When had that happened?

Music still played, but it was turned down so low she could barely hear it. Damon waved at her, and she nodded. "I'll be right back, Harper. No one will bother you." She didn't mention that it looked like everyone had left.

Tessa strode over to Damon.

"How is she?" he asked.

"Okay. The bullwhip is a hard limit."

"I know." Damon ran his hand through his hair. "Did she say anything about why Peter would do this?"

Tessa shook her head. "Harper said they talked about the scene before starting, but when they got ready to start, he wanted to use the bullwhip, and she said no."

"She called out her safe word," Damon said.

Tessa nodded. "I suspect Peter was arguing with her, and she knew that was a way to get him to listen. She really

127

didn't say."

Damon pulled in a harsh breath through his teeth. "This is a mess. Peter is saying she agreed, then backed out."

"So?" Tessa put her hands on her hips. "That's her right."

"I agree." Damon grinned. "Don't get all prissy on me."

Tessa's hackles rose. "I'll show you prissy."

"Later. After you've been punished for not doing as I told you."

Tessa lifted her chin. "Harper needed another sub, not a Dominant."

"That may be, but you were told to stay in that chair." Damon kept his voice low.

"We can't leave her alone," Sierra's voice carried over to them.

"Honey," Max started.

"Don't *honey* me." Sierra turned and stomped over to where Harper was sitting.

"Oh that doesn't sound good," Tessa said, watching her friend.

"Nope."

"You men are impossible." Crystal's voice rang out before she left the men staring after her as she went over to Sierra.

"I better see what is going on." Tessa made her way back to her friends and Harper. "Okay, you two, spill."

"Max and Jordan are trying to figure this all out," Sierra said, huffing out a breath.

"You're annoyed. What is going on?" Tessa asked.

"I want to take Harper home with us, but Max refused."

"So then I said Harper could come to my place with me, and Jordan had a fit."

"Doesn't Harper live with Peter?"

"No, they're play partners," Sierra said.

"Why did everyone leave?" Tessa wondered about that.

"It's almost two, and the few that were left were watching, not playing, so Max shut the club down early."

"Makes sense. I think Max and Jordan want you to themselves that's why they're refusing." Max and Jordan were a little controlling when they thought it was best for their women. Tessa had observed it enough to know these men took protection of their women seriously.

"Yes, but Harper needs support. Peter is lying," Sierra said.

Tessa agreed. "Why don't we do this: I was planning to go home tonight; she can come with me, and you two can make your men happy."

"What about Damon?" Crystal asked.

"What about him? We never agreed to spend tonight together." They hadn't. Maybe it was implied, but plans had changed.

"I'm really all right," Harper said.

"You don't need to be alone. And it's just for one night," Tessa said.

"I like that compromise, as long as you won't get into trouble with Damon," Sierra said.

"I'm already in trouble, so don't sweat it."

"This is your first night playing together at the club, and you're in trouble?" Crystal's voice held astonishment."

"Yeah. Damon told me to stay sitting in the chair, but when I saw Harper, I knew she needed the comfort of another sub."

"Well, you've been in the lifestyle longer than any of us," Sierra said.

"I've witnessed more," Tessa clarified.

"I don't want anyone to get into trouble or go to any trouble," Harper piped up. "I'm okay."

Tessa studied the woman. Her skin was back to a normal color, her blue eyes bright, and she smiled; it was a sad but genuine smile.

"You are looking better," Crystal said.

"I'm good." Harper rose. "Really, I appreciate the support, but I want to go home."

"Did you drive?" Sierra asked.

"Yes."

"Let one of us drive you home at least. We can make sure you get your car tomorrow." Tessa threw out there.

"That I will not say no to." Harper smiled.

"Okay, let me go talk to the guys and figure out who will take Harper home," Tessa said.

"Probably me and Jordan," Crystal said. "I believe Harper lives in one of the lofts in town."

"Not too far from Lara's cafe."

"So that makes Jordan and me the closest, since Max's home is next door, and Damon lives out here as well," Crystal said.

"How do you know that?" Tessa put her hands on her hips.

"Down, girl." Crystal gave a laugh. "Jordan dropped off some supplies Damon needed last week, and I was with him."

Tessa shook her head. What was wrong with her? Crystal had Jordan; in fact, she was very much in love with Jordan. "Sorry, I must be tired." She rubbed her forehead.

"It's okay, my friend." Crystal touched Tessa's arm.

"Well, now that's settled." Sierra looked across the room. "Looks like the men have taken care of Peter. Shall we go tell them our plans."

"Let's."

* * * *

Thirty minutes later, Tessa sat back against the leather seat in Damon's car. She pulled in a deep breath and let out slowly. "I'm exhausted."

"It is almost three in the morning."

"Ugh." She really didn't want to drive home tonight, nor did she want Damon to make the trek to her apartment and then back to his house. "Are you still mad at me?"

"Never mad. Annoyed maybe, but never mad. You did something out of the goodness of your heart, not because you wanted to disobey me."

"Thank you." She was surprised he understood that.

"But I'm still going to punish you," he remarked, pulling into his garage.

"Oh?" She'd kind of hoped he'd forgotten about that.

Damon grinned at her as he opened her door and helped her out. "I don't forget."

Tessa's heart pounded as they entered the house. What did he have planned for her?

"Let's see. I'll make this easy, go into the bedroom and undress. I'll be there in a moment."

Tessa nodded and made her way to his bedroom. Her heart pounded with each step she took. The rich masculine colors soothed her nerves as she undressed and waited, her stomach churning with butterflies.

* * * *

Damon waited until Tessa was in the bedroom before he put his bag in the closet and closed the door. He wasn't going to punish her in a true sense. A short spanking would remind her that he was to be obeyed in the club.

He spoke the truth when he said he understood why she did what she did. Harper was having a hard time talking

131

with him. It happened sometimes with a sub and a Dom, even though the subs all knew him.

They were going to need to figure out a better support system for both the Doms and subs. Peter was contrite about what he did, and promised to apologize to Harper. He admitted he hadn't listened to her when she went over her hard limits.

What a mess. Five years into this and things were starting to slowly unravel. Had the club grown too big? That was another thing they needed to discuss tomorrow. Figuring he'd given Tessa enough time. He made his way into the bedroom.

He stopped in his tracks. Tessa was kneeling in front of the bed, her head down so her chestnut hair cascaded over her shoulders. Her hands were on her thighs. Her total submission to him was a gift, one that overwhelmed him. They'd known each other such a short time, and here she was submitting to him.

"Tessa," he said, then groaned. "Sweetheart." Damon was never at a loss for words, but her submissive position sliced into his heart. "Please stand up."

"I did something wrong, Sir." She didn't move an inch.

"Something minor." Damon walked over to her and held out his hand. "Please." She lifted her head in response to his plea, and he gently grasped her offered hand as she rose from her knees, helping her to stand. "You never have to kneel for me."

Tessa blinked at him; her brown eyes held confusion.

"Come here." He tugged her over to the bed. "While I know a lot of Doms enjoy having their women at their feet, I'm not one of them."

"Yes, Sir."

Damon shook his head. "Believe my words, Tessa. I

don't want you kneeling on the floor in our bedroom or in the club. I might want you to sit on the floor and lean on my legs at the club, but that would be the extent of it. Understand?"

"I do, Sir."

"Good. Now on your hands and knees on the bed. It's time for your punishment."

She sighed and climbed onto the mattress in the position he asked for. "This for leaving your seat in the club when I told you to stay there."

"Yes, Sir." Tessa dropped her head.

Damon rubbed her ass, watching her skin flush. Then he raised his hand and brought it down.

"Ohhhh." She'd shifted her body down but then rose back up.

"Good girl." He rubbed the area he'd smacked before he did it again on her other ass cheek. This time she didn't move. By the fourth smack, Tessa was moaning. "Two more," he said and rapidly landed them, before rubbing her ass. It was hot, but he hadn't hit her hard. Enough to get his point across.

Damon stripped off his clothes and climbed onto the mattress. "Come here." He held his arms open.

Tessa climbed up over his body until she was lying on top of him, her head on his chest, her legs tangling with his. "Such a good girl. How are you doing?"

"I'm fine, Sir."

"Drop the sir. I don't need it right now." He stroked her back and ass, feeling the heat from his spanking. "Your skin is hot."

"I'm not surprised," she said. "I feel like every nerve in my body has moved into my butt."

"The blood flow has increased in the area. I want to

know how you felt about the spanking?"

Tessa tilted her head up. "Are you asking me if I liked it?"

"Yes."

"It was different." She bit her lip in concentration. "You weren't heavy handed, but I did feel it."

"Have you been spanked before?" Why hadn't he thought to ask that question before?

"Once, but nothing like this." She snuggled up to him. "You were holding back, weren't you?"

"A bit. I understood why you left your seat. You saw a sub in need, and you reacted."

"That I did."

"So your punishment was light. Further defiance will mean harsher punishments."

"I understand." Her head dropped to his shoulder. "Will Harper be okay?"

"I believe so. She was upset but not traumatized."

"I'll never forget Brady's face when Crystal brought him to my house."

"How did you get caught up in that?" He'd wondered about it since she said she'd met Sage during the whole court thing.

"Brady needed a place to stay for a few days where no one would find him. Crystal knew I had an extra bedroom, and no one would put us together."

"I'm glad you helped Brady and Sage. That was not a good situation."

"I'm sorry they had to go through all that trouble. Brady is such a nice man. We talked a lot, and I think it helped him and me."

"How did it help you?" Now he was really curious. Brady was good guy, but he was a sub through and through at the club.

"By talking about the relationship he had with Sage and how he feels when he's with her. He helped me realize the part of me that was missing was the playtime I could have with a Dom I trusted."

"And you trust me?" Damon was humbled.

"If I didn't, we wouldn't be here." Tessa rose up, using her hand on his chest as a brace. "Damon, if I didn't trust you on a basic level, we wouldn't be having this conversation. And I wouldn't have let you spend the night in my apartment."

"I remember when you didn't like me." He tucked a strand of her hair behind her ear.

She grinned. "That was more about you being an overprotective Neanderthal than dislike."

"Neanderthal? Those are fighting words." He rolled her onto her back.

Tessa chortled. "I like this fight."

Damon covered her lips with his.

CHAPTER NINE

Damon pulled up to Max's house, unable to stop smiling. Last night with Tessa had been really good. She'd taken her punishment, such as it was, and they'd spent the night in each other's arms.

He should be worried that this couldn't last, but he wasn't. She hadn't run when he said he made adult toys, and she'd never questioned where he got his money. Usually that was the first thing women asked him upon seeing his home.

Lord knows his ex-girlfriends had, and none of them could deal with his dominant side. He rang the doorbell.

Max opened the door. "Hey, Damon. We're out back by the pool. Beer?"

"Yeah." Damon slipped off his shoes and made his way toward the patio. "Hey, Jordan."

"Hey."

Jordan was already sitting at the patio table with his laptop open. Damon had pen and paper; it helped him think when they had these meetings.

"Here you go." Max set a bottle of beer in front of him.

"I can't believe we've got such a nice day in March that we can sit out here," Max commented.

It was nice today. He'd commented on the weather to Tessa this morning when he walked her to her car, given her a hard kiss and instructions to not go too crazy with Sierra and Crystal.

"I like it," Jordan commented.

"Shall we get business out of the way?" Max asked.

"Yeah." Damon looked down at the notes he'd made on his phone. "I think maybe the first thing is we're going to need more help at the club."

* * * *

"So what happened last night after you left the club?" Crystal was curled up on one end of her sofa.

"Was Damon mad you disobeyed him?" Sierra asked.

Tessa took a sip of water. "He wasn't mad. I think I disappointed him on some level, but he understood why I did it. As for what happened, a nice spanking and cuddle time." Her cheeks warmed.

She didn't know why. She really wasn't embarrassed. These were her friends. Heck, she'd seen Sierra half undressed last night.

"Nice," Sierra commented.

"Why did you disobey Damon?" Crystal asked.

"Harper needed the support of another sub." Her friends stared at her. "Sierra, it was like when you stood up for Regina."

"That was because Samantha was going to hit her. You didn't think Damon was going to hurt Harper?" Sierra's voice held a note of horror.

"No, no, no. Damon would never strike a woman." That was instinct talking, but she'd watched him last night before she approached. He was very respectful of Harper's personal space. "It's something I picked up on at the DC clubs I used to attend. Some subs have difficulty opening up to a Dom, especially after an incident with one."

"I never thought of that," Sierra said.

"So much to learn," Crystal muttered.

"It takes time. Both of you mingle with the subs, so it's a matter of getting to know them better."

"But how?" Sierra asked. "I've probably been in the

137

club the longest of the three of us, well, except you, Tessa. You've been a member longer than any of us."

"I have. Cut yourselves a break. Sierra, you've only been with Max for a few months, Crystal barely two months. I've been in the lifestyle since college." Except for that several year hiatus she'd happily ended. Tessa sighed with the contentment that filled her.

"Tell us more." Sierra sat forward.

In that moment, Tessa realized she'd never really clued her friends into her life. "I'm sorry I've kept things from the two of you." Tessa ducked her head.

"Hey, none of that." Crystal's tone was firm. "We've all kept stuff private."

"I know." She looked at her friends. "I'm sorry I wasn't as supportive as I should have been while you two were first learning about the lifestyle. I had such mixed feelings about it."

"What made you change your mind?" Sierra asked.

"Both of you and Brady." They laughed, but Tessa was serious. "Really. After having been told I was sick, I tried to play here, but nothing seemed right."

"You love reading the racy books," Crystal commented.

"I do. They were a lifeline for me. Keeping me safe while still getting to experience kink." Tessa thought about the books she had stashed away in her bedroom. Her private collection. Would her friends be shocked?

"You got us into reading them," Sierra said. "I don't think I would have been as brave with Max if you hadn't."

"Same with Jordan. Even though it started out as part of the case, I didn't go in blind."

"I'm glad." And she was. "So anyway, my choice to disobey Damon was because I was concerned about Harper.

He understood that, but I also understood his need to punish me for not staying where he told me to."

"Max hasn't ever really disciplined me. It's more pleasure than pain."

"Same with Jordan."

"The spanking did seem to be more about discipline than inflicting pain." Tessa tilted her head and looked at her friends. "The thing is, Damon listened. He didn't jump to conclusions or anything. Many times in the DC scene, I saw Doms jump to conclusions and punish their sub when really a little more communication could have prevented or solved what seemed to be a minor problems."

"That is one nice thing. Our men listen to us," Sierra said.

"I've noticed that with most of the Doms in the club; they do listen. There are some exceptions," Crystal said.

"There are always exceptions, but the guys seem good at weeding out those who may have issues." Tessa had been surprised and liked how they did that. "So now that all that is out of the way, what's on tap?"

"I say we go surprise the men." Sierra jumped up.

"Aren't they having a business meeting?" Tessa wasn't so sure this was a good idea.

"So what?" Crystal chimed in. "It's such a nice day for the beginning of March. I want to get outside."

"Then let's go take a walk or something," Tessa suggested.

"I think someone is afraid of Damon," Sierra teased.

Tessa almost said, "am not" like a kid. She wasn't afraid of Damon; she didn't want any further punishments, and there was no guessing how the guys would react if they showed up without notice. "How about we call first?"

"That will ruin the surprise." Sierra crossed her arms

over her chest.

There was no reasoning with Sierra when she was in this mood. "Let me go to the bathroom first." Tessa slipped into the bathroom. Her friends could get mad at her later. She pulled out her phone and texted Damon.

* * * *

"We're going to have company," Damon said with a smile.

"What?" Max looked up from the financials they were studying.

"Tessa texted me they're on their way out here."

Max and Jordan pulled their phones out and shook their heads. "Nothing from Sierra."

"Nor from Crystal."

"What are they up to?" Max asked.

"And why did Tessa warn you? She had to know you'd tell us," Jordan commented.

Damon wondered about that as well. "It might have to do with my disciplining her last night."

Max and Jordan grinned. "How did that go?" Jordan asked.

"It was more of a reinforcement of the rules, to be honest. I only spanked her six times, enough to get my point across."

"That's what I'll need to do with Sierra. She knows better than to do something like this."

"Same with Crystal. How are we going to play this?"

The men went silent for a moment, then Max grinned. "Let them think they got away with it." He tapped his fingers on the table. "Then we pounce."

Jordan rubbed his hands together. "They'll learn not to surprise their Doms when they've been told it's a business meeting."

Damon shook his head. "I won't punish Tessa. She told me."

"Of course not," Max said. "I'll take Sierra into the bedroom. Jordan your choice of office or the club."

"I can use the office. All I need is a chair or a table. A desk will work too. It might be fun to use a ruler."

"Oh, those two are in for it," Damon said.

"We Doms need to keep them in line. They knew this was a business meeting, not a get-together to shoot the bull." Max stood up. "I'm going to go get some things ready. Damon, if you're interested, there's a nice shady place right past those trees." Max pointed past the pool. "You and Tessa can explore a little nature while you're here."

"Now that sounds delightful. Do you have a blanket and pillows?"

"Coming right up." Max disappeared into the house, then came back out with the items. "Jordan, you need anything?"

"No. I'm going to clear an area on your desk." Jordan stood.

"Ruler in the top hand drawer, and there is also a metal one."

"Excellent." Jordan's eyes gleamed with anticipation.

Damon shook his head as his two friends walked into the house. The afternoon had taken an intriguing twist.

* * * *

Sierra unlocked the front door to her and Max's home, signaling her friends to be quiet. But the house was already silent.

"They must be out by the pool," Sierra whispered as they took off their shoes. She motioned for them to follow.

"This isn't a good idea," Tessa cautioned once again.

141

She'd tried to get them to text or call during the entire drive out, or to let her. But both had their minds made up. Neither one of them seemed to realize how much trouble they were about to get into. Or maybe they did?

"Yep, out by the pool," Sierra whispered. The trio crossed the family room to the open patio doors. "One, two, three."

"Surprise!" Sierra and Crystal yelled, and they bounced out the door.

The men stood up, Max and Jordan's expressions concealed. Damon smiled at her and held out his hand. Tessa didn't hesitate. She went over and put her hand in his.

"What is the meaning of this?" Max's voice was hard and cold, so cold that Tessa shivered.

"A surprise," Sierra whispered.

"What did I tell you we were doing today?" Max crossed his arms over his chest, looking down at Sierra.

"Club business." Her voice was so soft Tessa could barely hear her.

"What do you have to say for yourself?" Jordan's voice was as hard and cold as Max's. Tessa saw Crystal's head fall forward.

"I'm sorry," she whispered.

"Sierra, into our bedroom. You have two minutes to get your ass in there and strip."

Sierra didn't hesitate. She took off at a run with Max following her.

"Let's go." Jordan grasped Crystal by the arm.

"Are we going home?" Crystal asked.

"No, but we're going to make use of Max's office." Jordan and Crystal disappeared into the house.

Damon tugged Tessa into his arms. "Thanks for the warning."

"I feel bad that Sierra and Crystal are in trouble." She snuggled up against him, enjoying the feel of his arms around her.

"Did you try and stop them?"

"Yes."

"Did you try and convince them to call or text?"

"I did."

"Then don't feel bad."

A cry reached the patio doors, and Tessa stiffened. "I can't hear this."

"Come on." Damon released her from his embrace and led her past the pool out into the trees. It was cooler here. Even though there'd been shade on the patio, this was much cooler. He led her to a small clearing, in the center a blanket and pillows.

Tessa stepped into the clearing and looked up. The tall trees created a natural shelter, and the grass was green and soft. "This is beautiful."

"Max told me about it. So we have our own little place while they take care of business."

Damon tugged Tessa down onto the blanket. "I know they won't hurt them, but that cry was Crystal."

"Are you asking me what Jordan is doing?"

"Not really. Part of me wants to know, but the other doesn't. I just...I don't know." She shrugged. "I want to protect them."

"My tender little Tessa." Damon pulled her into his arms and lay back. "Lie here with me and enjoy nature."

"We're not going to act like randy teenagers and make out?"

"I didn't say that."

* * * *

An hour later, voices penetrated their little slice of

heaven. "I guess we should go back," Damon said.

"Yes." Tessa stood. She helped Damon fold the blanket and pick up the pillows. When they walked out of the trees, her friends gaped at her. Sierra and Crystal were dressed, color high in their cheeks, and their clothing was mussed.

"Well, now that we've taken care of that business…" Max announced.

"I think it's time to call for pizza," Jordan suggested.

"You're reading my mind." Max picked up his phone and made the call.

"Sit down, sweetheart. I'll go put these in the house." Damon took the pillows from her.

"Okay." Tessa sat down, but her gaze stayed on Damon as he walked inside. Damn, that man had a fine ass.

"Traitor," Sierra whispered.

"What did we talk about, Sierra?" Max had finished his call and was glaring at Sierra.

"Sorry, Tessa. And I remember, Max. Trust me."

"We should have called or texted," Crystal said. "Tessa was the bright one." She shifted on her chair and grimaced.

"I…" Tessa ducked her head. "I'm sorry both of you got into trouble." She hated this feeling of guilt. She'd done the right thing, but someone suffered for it. Wasn't that the story of her life.

"Oh, honey." Sierra reached over and took her hand. "It was our own fault. It really was. I don't blame you for texting Damon."

"I don't either," Crystal said.

"You shouldn't blame yourself." Jordan stood up and walked over to her. "You take too much on your shoulders, Tessa." He rested a hand on her shoulder.

Max walked over to where she sat, and without a word, he pulled her out of the chair into his arms. "We didn't hurt them, merely reminded them who's boss. Don't fret."

His softly spoken words helped her heart lighten.

"Hey, why are you hugging my woman?" Damon said, walking out of the house.

"She needed it." Max released her and stepped back.

Tessa 'fessed up. "I was blaming myself for the situation."

Damon stared at her with his arms crossed over his chest. Instead of being intimidated, a shaft of anticipation ran up Tessa's spine. Damon acted tough, but he could be marshmallow inside.

"Pizza has been ordered. Who wants what to drink?" Max asked. Orders were placed, and by the time the pizza arrived, they were all talking and laughing.

CHAPTER TEN

On Wednesday afternoon, Tessa drove to Damon's house. She had the afternoon off, and it was book club night, so Damon asked her to come out to his place. They'd have an early dinner then go together. She kept trying to convince him he didn't have to cook for her, but he insisted. And who was she to deny him? Besides, she loved watching him move around in his kitchen and the way his muscles played along his back. Her man looked good in an apron.

She smiled. Her man. Yes, Damon was hers. It had been a month since the Valentine's Day party, but they'd spent a lot of time together. Her phone rang, and she automatically answered on hands free.

"Hello."

"Hello, sis."

"Allen." Tessa almost swerved her car off the road. Why was her brother calling?

"I'm going to be out West in a few weeks. Why don't we have dinner?"

Tessa blinked. "Dinner?" She'd visited her family a few times but kept a super low profile. She didn't want anything to follow her back here, to her home.

"Yeah, you know… Dinner. Food. Conversation."

"Sure. I guess." What else could she say to her brother?

"Okay, good. I'll call when I get to town. Bye." The line went dead. Tessa turned down Damon's driveway and stopped. Her brother was coming to town. She wondered why. She'd have to check political news and see if there was something big going on. She couldn't see him simply coming to see her.

Pushing thoughts of her brother out of her head, Tessa continued up the driveway and parked. She knocked on the front door, but there was no answer. She pulled out her cell phone and called him.

"Damon, here." He sounded out of breath.

"It's Tessa. I'm at the house."

"Aw, shit. Sorry, I got caught up in work. Look toward the garage, see that path?"

"Yes."

"Take it and you'll come around to my workshop. The doors are open, so just walk in."

"Okay." Tessa ended the call. She'd been curious about his workshop. Now, she'd get to see it. She stashed her purse back in her car and pushed her cell into the front pocket of her jeans before making her way down the path to Damon's workshop.

As she got closer, grunge music blared. She wondered how Damon could even think, but then she saw him striking a piece of metal with a hammer. The smell of hot iron hung in the air.

Damon glanced up. "Hi," he said, but she put her hand to her ear.

He turned down the music. "Sorry, forgot I had it so loud." He banged on the metal a few more times before he lifted it with metal tongs and dunked it into another bucket filled with water.

She looked around his workshop. "Wow."

"Is that a good wow or bad wow?" he asked, wiping his face with a surprisingly clean white towel.

"Good wow." This is amazing. She glanced around at the metal pieces hung around the shop.

"Thanks. All the metal is a special order from a client who is doing suspension and wants different shapes and sizes to use."

"You made all of these?" Tessa ran her fingers over the entwined metal circles sitting on the workbench all polished up.

"Yep." Damon captured her hand and lifted it to his lips. "I thought I'd be finished before you came out tonight."

"No worries." She watched him start shutting down his equipment. Then his computer pinged.

"Can you take a look at that? It's an incoming email."

"Sure." Tessa crossed to the desk. While it wasn't messy, there were drawings all over it. Sitting down in the chair, she clicked the email open. "Someone named Dave wants to know if you can make him your special double-headed vibrator and a set of silver nipple rings?"

"Would you reply for me and tell him yes, but it will take at least three weeks. I'm swamped right now."

Tessa typed out the message and sent it. That's when she noticed his inbox. There were at least one hundred messages in it. "It looks like you're busy."

"Yeah. A few months ago a club in San Francisco contacted me about making a few things for their annual exhibition. I did. It was held two weeks ago, and the orders have been pouring in since then."

"Impressive." How famous was Damon? "Are all your orders from there?"

"No. I've made specialized stuff for clubs in New York, Chicago, Texas, Florida, and DC." He strode over to the desk. "Most of my stuff goes to Doms. But the clubs are starting to ask for stuff to show. So word has gotten around."

"By the tone of your voice, I'm not sure if you think it's a good thing or not."

"A little of both." He motioned her out of the chair, then shut down the computer. They walked out, and he locked up the workshop. "I like my work, but I never wanted to be famous or anything."

"Is that what's happening?" A twinge of worry tensed Tessa's shoulders. How famous would he get?

"A little bit. But I'm not stressing about it. No one has to meet me in person. I do everything via email."

"No internet store?" He could do one so easily.

"Nope. Too much trouble." He opened the door, and they walked into his home. "Go relax in the family room while I take a shower."

"What were you planning for dinner?" she asked before he walked down the hall.

"Shrimp, pasta, and a salad." He disappeared.

Tessa padded to the kitchen and opened the fridge. The least she could do was get stuff started for him. Finding a big pot, she added water and put it on the stove. Then she found a chopping board and a knife and began chopping items for the salad.

Doing this type of repetitive work gave her a few moments to sort out what she was feeling about Damon's work. Maybe she was making a mountain out of a pile of dirt. He said he did everything via email. He didn't really meet people, so even knowing his name didn't mean anything. She wasn't part of that and wouldn't be involved, or known, because of it. Yet the coils of fear snaked their way around her heart.

She looked up as Damon came into the room, rubbing his hair dry, shirtless. Her mouth watered, and she pushed her misgivings away.

149

"You didn't need to start chopping," he said, dropping a kiss on her cheek.

He smelled like pine and a fresh spring day. "I figured I might as well help."

"Thank you." He stepped out and down the hall. When he came back, the towel was gone. He pulled the shrimp from the fridge.

"How was the job today?" he asked.

"Same old, same old. I've been working on the collections this week. Trying to figure out what I can spend and where." She loved collections, but it was hard. Patrons had been asking for more continuing stories, and most times, there wasn't the budget for all of it.

"I think my education may be lacking. Sounds like you can't buy everything you want for the library."

"That is correct. I have a budget, and it's not big. My patrons want stuff, but I can't get it all, so I have to pick and choose."

"I see." He put the pasta in the water. "Would more money help?"

Tessa snorted, then laughed. "Yes, but since all the money is funneled through the county, I doubt I'd get that much. But don't get me wrong. I love my job. I sometimes wish the bureaucrats understood how important libraries are."

"Enlighten me some more."

Tessa finished up with the salad, washed her hands, and put the salad back in the fridge to keep cool. "Are you sure you want to hear this?"

"I do." Damon leaned against the counter.

"Okay, for example, we only have four computers. So we have to limit the time both kids and adults want to use them."

"Don't kids have computers at home?"

"Not all. Not all have internet either." Another sore point. She'd lobbied her father for years to work on bills that helped those that needed it. Her pleas fell on deaf ears, or at least, that's what it felt like.

"I didn't realize." He stirred the pasta.

"It's a struggle at times. But I make it work."

Damon nodded. "Can you get the strainer; it's next to the sink under the silverware drawer."

Tessa pulled it out and placed it in the sink. "What do you want to drink with dinner?" She moved the conversation on to better things.

* * * *

Tessa pulled into the parking lot of his bookstore. Damon noticed there were a lot more cars tonight. He climbed out of the vehicle and helped Tessa out.

"Is it me or does it look busier?" she said.

"It's not you." Damon guided her to the store and opened the door. Chaos.

"Oh thank goodness, you're early," Destiny said from behind the counter.

Damon stared at all the people. "What do you need?"

"There are a couple of guys in back looking for something special, another guy had a question about restraints, and there were some others I can't remember right now."

"On it." Damon looked down at her.

"Go." She waved her hands, then squeezed between two people in line with an excuse me and rounded the counter. "What can I do to help you?"

"Bag, please."

"You got it."

An hour later, Damon was pleased to see the line down

to a few people, but the book club room was almost full. He put signs on seats in the back for his friends.

"I don't understand. What happened?" Damon asked. Yes, the store made a good profit, but they had never been as busy as they were tonight.

"My fault," Destiny said. "I thought maybe it would be a good idea to advertise the book club a little bit, so I had it put into the "What's Happening" section of the online newspaper."

"It caused all this?" Tessa asked.

"Apparently. I'm guessing people were afraid to come in here, but when they saw the ad, they felt better about it."

"I get that. I remember when I first found out about the book club being in an adult shop, I wasn't sure."

"You weren't?" Damon looked down at her.

"No. But Damon, your store isn't what most of us think an adult store is like."

"What do you mean?"

"She means those sleazy stores, with booths in the back, old geezers with pot bellies getting off, and in a part of town no one wants to visit," Destiny said.

"I guess I never thought about it. I wanted something where people feel comfortable."

"And that's why it's getting so popular." Tessa smiled at him.

"Yeah, and I noticed something as we came in. I'm going to make a quick phone call." Damon stepped outside the store. The building next to him was empty with a For Sale sign in the window. He called the number listed.

Damon had just hung up the phone when Max, Sierra, Jordan, and Crystal arrived. "What is going on? The parking lot is almost full." Max asked.

"We've got a full house tonight. I'll explain later."

They all traipsed inside. Damon didn't want to lock the door, but he changed the sign to *Closed – Book Club In Progress* and went in back.

Destiny was at the front of the book club group, but Damon decided to stay by the doorway in case someone walked in.

The book club lasted longer than ever. With new people, there was a lot of conversation. They sold out of the chosen book in record time. It was almost eleven before they got everyone out of the store.

"I think your advertisement went too well," Damon said to Destiny.

"Yeah, but we made record money tonight." She smiled.

Damon glanced at his watch. He told Tessa and his friends he'd meet them at the coffee shop, but that was an hour ago.

"Go meet everyone, Damon. I'll lock up."

"Are you sure?"

"Yes, boss, I'm sure." Destiny all but pushed him out the door. She locked the door and turned the sign to Closed once again.

Damon made his way to the coffee shop, happy to see his friends still there, chatting away.

"About time," Jordan said.

"Sorry." Damon leaned down and brushed a kiss over Tessa's lips. "I never expected us to get that busy."

"It's a good thing," Sierra commented.

"It's wonderful." Damon took his seat.

"Americano?" a woman said next to Damon.

"That's his," Tessa said.

The cup was set in front of him. He smiled his thanks at the server before he took a long sip. "Thanks, sweetheart," Damon said to Tessa.

"I told her earlier that, when you joined us, to bring it over. I didn't expect you to be so late."

"Me either. Are you going to be okay at work tomorrow?"

"It will be fine."

"Aw, aren't they sweet," Tessa remarked.

Damon glanced over to see Crystal had her head on Jordan's shoulder. Then he looked back at Tessa.

Max cleared his throat. "Since we're all here, Zeke came out and looked at what I want to have done."

"And?" Damon leaned forward.

"He can do it. The thing is the cost." Max leaned back in his chair.

"That much?" Jordan asked.

"Actually, it's better than I thought it would be. Zeke figures around two hundred thousand total."

"That's not bad," Damon said. He'd figured more. "So roughly about sixty-seven thousand from each of us."

"Yes. Zeke is willing to work with half up front and half at completion," Max said.

"That works for me," Jordan said.

"Me too." Damon knew he had enough money to cover the expansion of the club and buy the retail space next to his store. Not that he was going to pay cash for the space. He'd finance it. But he didn't have any worries at all.

"You guys have that kind of money sitting around?" Tessa asked, amazement in her voice.

Sierra laughed. "Did I forget to tell you? Max has money."

"Jordan owns the law firm, and Sierra and I contribute to all the household stuff, even if they don't want us to," Crystal commented.

Tessa looked at Damon. "Don't fret, Tessa. I'm fine." How would she feel when she found out he had money? He'd find out soon enough, once he talked to the real estate agent, and later Zeke. Already in his head, Damon could see the wall between the two shops demolished and the business expanding into the next building.

He was already deciding to make the next building more of a bookshop. A place where they could hold the book club meetings and sell all sorts of books. He was limited on how many books he could carry in his current store, but with more space, there were possibilities, especially since they were talking about more education for members of the club.

"Since we're all in agreement, I'll have Zeke get a contract drawn up." Max held up his hand. "I'll let you read it, Jordan. All three of us will have to sign it anyway."

Jordan laughed. "Right."

"So what do we have here?" A female voice intruded as a flash went off.

Jordan rose to his feet, and Crystal groaned. "You're disturbing us. Please go away."

Max put his arm around Sierra's shoulders, and Damon leaned closer to Tessa.

"Now, Mr. Frost. What are you hiding?"

Max narrowed his eyes. "Just friends having coffee. Nothing to hide here." Max's voice was ice cold.

"Friends who have coffee after being at a book club meeting at an adult store. My readers will find that very interesting, especially since I've done some research." The woman turned to Max. "I understand you own a business called Wicked Sanctuary."

Sierra sat up, and Tessa stiffened next to Damon. Damon rose to his feet next to Jordan. "Miss…"

"Collins. Shantell Collins." Her voice went all breathy and soft.

Damon had dealt with this type of woman before. Thought they could distract a man with their looks. In addition, he'd heard her name before. She was the reporter who'd made Jordan and Crystal's life difficult during Sage's court case.

"Ms. Collins," Damon started. "Why don't we take a walk outside." He took her by the arm and began leading her away from his friends. Once outside, he kept his smile. "Why are you bothering us?" His tone was cold and hard.

"I am a reporter."

"I don't care. We're private citizens, living our lives." He wasn't going to give this woman anything about them.

"Really? Mr. Frost and Ms. Hayden recently defended a woman accused of abuse."

"The case was dismissed. I'm sure lawyers defend abuse cases every day." Damon kept a straight face, never raising his voice.

"This is different." She slid closer to Damon, and it took everything he had not to take a step back from her cloying perfume. "I understand the couple he was defending are into some freaky stuff."

Damon swore silently. They were all aware that a lot of information was publicly accessible. The last thing they needed was some nosy reporter in their lives. "That case is over and has nothing to do with us." He stepped to the side. "I would appreciate you leaving us alone."

"And if I don't?"

"Then expect a restraining order from my lawyer." Damon went back inside the coffee shop.

Jordan was talking softly to Crystal, as was Tessa. Max and Sierra were in a quiet conversation.

"I hate that woman," Crystal said.

"She was fishing," Damon said, and all eyes turned to him.

"What did she say?" Max asked.

"Nothing much. Mentioned Sage and Brady's case, but that was it." He went over to Tessa and pulled her to his side. Her lips were pressed tightly together. Was she upset because the reporter got a picture? He tucked her tighter to his side. "She's nothing."

"But she can cause trouble." Sierra looked up at Max. "She knows the name of the club."

"Public record. I have a business license and a liquor license, even though we don't use that," Max said.

"There's really nothing she can do but search public records. Everything we've done is legal," Jordan said. "I should know. I made sure all the paperwork was executed properly."

"We've never tried to hide that it's a private club, and we don't talk about who we see there," Damon added.

"Do you think this will hurt business?" Sierra asked.

"What is she going to print? Pleasant Valley has a BDSM club?" Max snickered. "Hell, we'd most likely be overrun with people."

Sierra laughed. "You're probably right."

"I wouldn't worry. I told her if she continued to harass us, she'd find herself with a restraining order," Damon said.

"No reporter wants that," Crystal said, then yawned.

"That's my cue," Jordan said. "We both have work in the morning."

"Yeah, we should be going too," Max said.

"Max, catch a ride to my place?" Damon asked.

"Sure."

They left the coffee house, and thankfully, the reporter

was gone. "Give me a minute," Damon said to Max. Damon walked Tessa to her car. "Dinner Friday?"

"I'd like that, but come to my place. I can cook."

"All right." He drew her against him. His body reacted. "Are you okay?"

"Why wouldn't I be?"

"The reporter?"

"She didn't upset me. I was more concerned with everyone else."

Damon wasn't so sure. Her shoulders were still stiff. But now wasn't the time to confront her. Not in front of their friends. "All right. Until tomorrow night at the club." Damon lowered his head. The second his lips touched hers, Tessa parted her mouth so he could explore. He tasted the chocolate in the mocha she'd had at the coffee shop.

He didn't want to break the kiss. His dick was pulsing, wanting more. He wanted more. But not tonight. She had work tomorrow and so did he.

"Damon," she whispered when he lifted his head.

"I know. But you need to work." He opened her car door. "Drive home safely and call me once you're home."

"I will." She climbed behind the wheel. "Club tomorrow night and dinner Friday."

"I'll be there. And I'll bring dessert on Friday."

Tessa grinned as she shut the door, rolled down the window, and started her vehicle. "I thought I was dessert."

Before Damon could form an answer, she pulled out of her spot and drove out of the parking lot with a wave. Damon shook his head. He was going to have a boner all night now. He made his way to where Max's SUV was parked and climbed in the back seat.

"Thanks for the ride home. I didn't want Tessa to drive out and back."

"I'm surprised you didn't take her home with you," Max said, pulling out onto the street.

"She has work tomorrow, but I considered it."

Sierra turned in her seat. "Don't hurt my friend, Damon."

"I won't." He had no intentions of hurting Tessa. He was halfway in love with her. The thought should have scared him, but it didn't. He was finding Tessa was very different from other women. In a way, perfect for him.

* * * *

Friday evening, Tessa pushed her hair away from her face. Okay, maybe cooking for Damon wasn't one of her brightest ideas. She barely cooked for herself, and now she was cooking for him. To what? Impress him? Yeah, right. The recipe sounded so easy. Chicken Cordon Bleu. Her first problem had been pounding the chicken thin. She didn't have a meat mallet or a rolling pin. The recipe said you could use a heavy pot.

She pulled out her biggest pot. Her soup pot. Put the chicken between the sheets of plastic wrap and started smashing it with the pot. After a couple of minutes, she looked at the chicken. It still looked too big. Ugh. She tried again, and again.

Now, that looked better. She looked at the picture in the recipe, okay maybe not as thin as it looked in the picture but good enough. Tessa layered in the ham and Swiss cheese, then rolled. The darn things wouldn't stay rolled.

"Roll, you bastard. And stay that way."

Frustrated, she put a toothpick in them and followed the instructions to put them in plastic wrap and refrigerate. While the chicken cooled, she prepared the eggs, flour, and bread crumbs.

She glanced at the clock. Dang, it was already five-thirty. She read the rest of the recipe quickly. This shouldn't take too long. The timer dinged, and she took the chicken out of the fridge and unwrapped it.

Okay, dredge in flour, then the egg, and then breadcrumbs. She could do that. Except the chicken kept wanting to unroll. And what was she supposed to do with the chicken next? Crap! She forgot to put the oil in the pan.

Washing her hands, she grabbed a pan and poured in some olive oil and turned it on. She hated frying food, but she could do this. She placed the first piece of chicken in and jumped back as oil splattered.

"Damn it." Tessa blew out a frustrated breath. *Okay, let's get the next one in there.* She put the second one in, this time prepared for the splatter. Five minutes, then turn over. She set the timer and put the dishes in the sink.

Next was the sauce. Did they really need it? She decided they didn't. The timer went off and when she went to turn the chicken it unrolled. "Son of a…" Using a spatula she pulled it out of the pan and put on the cutting board and tried to roll it again.

"Fuck!" She almost burned herself. How the hell was she going to roll this? Her doorbell rang. "Just a second." She quickly washed her hands and went to the door. "Hey Damon, come in."

He looked at her, curiosity in his eyes, as the loud screech of the smoke alarm sounded. "Oh shit!" She ran for the kitchen. She'd forgotten about the other piece of chicken. Smoke was coming from the pan. She grabbed it and threw it into the sink and turned on the water, then turned off the burner.

Fresh air wafted into the kitchen, and she saw Damon standing by the window he'd opened. "Dinner?"

Tears sprang to her eyes, and she nodded. "I…" Her

160

voice wobbled. Couldn't she even cook him a meal?

"Honey." He enveloped her into his arms as she started to cry.

"I wanted so much to cook you dinner." Tessa was disappointed in herself. She should have stuck to the basics; instead, she tried to show off. Damon was always cooking for her and made it look so darn easy, and she couldn't even do a simple chicken recipe.

"It's okay." He rubbed her back.

"No, it's not." She leaned back in his arms. "That's what I get for wanting to cook for you. A colossal failure. That's me."

His features froze. "There are certain things I won't tolerate, and you calling yourself names is at the top of that list."

"But it's the truth." She tried to pull out of his arms, but he tightened his hold.

"Tessa," he started. "You are not a failure. The meal didn't work for you. It happens."

"Not to you."

He laughed. "Trust me, I've burned plenty of things." He leaned down and nuzzled her cheek. "I'll give you cooking lessons, if it's that important to you. I'm sure I can light your stove on fire."

"Stop." Laugher spilled from her lips. She stepped out of his embrace. "What a mess."

"What were you trying to make?"

"Chicken Cordon Bleu."

"What did you use to pound the chicken thin?" He glanced at the counter and the items now soaking in the sink.

"A pot. I don't have a mallet or rolling pin."

"Okay, do you have more ingredients for it?"

"Yes, I bought extra in case I screwed up, but I didn't think about how long it would take."

"Not long at all. First, let's clean up, and I'll walk you through how to make it."

Tessa shrugged, not really sure she wanted Chicken Cordon Bleu at all now. "Maybe we can go out to eat."

Damon grasped her around the waist and spun her to face him. "Together, we can do this. Come on, my spunky woman, where is your sense of adventure?"

His eyes twinkled, and Tessa's mood lightened. "All right. Everything is in the fridge, top shelf." Tessa threw out the burned food, scrubbed the pan, and put it back on the stove.

Damon set the ingredients out on the counter. "One of the tricks is to filet the chicken before you try to pound it." He pulled out one of her knives and fileted the meat. "Now it will be easier to get thin. I'll pound the chicken for you." He put the chicken in the wrap and pounded it with the pot.

Tessa sighed. Sure, he could do it. Look at those muscles flexing as he brought the pot down on the chicken. In no time, the breasts were flat and thin.

"I think that's where I went wrong. I didn't cut them in half, and I couldn't pound it hard enough."

"You probably needed to work at it a little longer. and I'll get you a mallet to use." He transferred the chicken onto a plate. "You do the layering."

She layered ham, cheese, ham, cheese, then looked up at Damon, who was right behind her.

"Now you roll it up." He put his arms around her and guided her hands to the chicken. "You want to roll it a little loose so it will stay." He instructed her.

A shiver went through Tessa's body with Damon's chest pressed against her back, his fingers directing hers.

Within a few minutes they had two perfectly rolled chicken breasts. Was the kitchen hotter than it had been? Sweat trickled between her breasts.

"Now, using the plastic wrap, put one piece in." He guided her once again. "Good, now grasp the ends of the wrap and twist it around."

Why did "twist it around" sound dirty to her? Maybe because she wanted to twist around and jump his bones. They were *cooking*. What was wrong with her that she couldn't stop thinking of sex? Oh yeah, they were cooking, all right. Tessa shook her head.

"See, now do the next one." She did. "Good. In the fridge they go for thirty minutes as the recipe calls for. Then we fry them."

"That seemed so simple." With him helping. She placed the chicken in the fridge.

"Only because I was here with you. Now what shall we do while we wait?" His eyebrows rose, and mischief danced in his eyes.

"I don't know." Her lips turned up. She looked down at herself. "Oh my goodness, I'm covered in flour and gunk. Yuck!" She pulled off her apron. At least it had protected her clothes.

"For what I'm thinking about, you don't need clothing." He picked up a bag and dangled it from his fingers.

"What is that?" She hadn't noticed him carrying anything when he walked in, but then she'd been a little distracted by the smoke alarm.

"Why don't we find out." Damon took her hand and led her to her bedroom. "I want to play. Are you ready?" he asked, holding up the bag.

"Yes." Her tongue darted out and wet her lips.

"Yes, what?"

"Yes, Sir." Tessa's tummy tightened. Was she ready for this? Damn right, she was. If they hadn't been interrupted in the club last week, and he hadn't had to work there last night... She blew out a breath.

"As part of our negotiation, are you okay with me using restraints and toys?"

"What do you have in mind, Sir?"

Damon stared at her. The mischief she'd seen in his gaze moments ago was even more pronounced now. "If I told you everything, what fun would that be?" He reached over and took her hand. "I won't push your limits tonight, only tease them a bit."

"I can handle that, Sir."

"Good." His hand slid up her arm, and his fingers curved around the back of her neck.

Instantly, her bones weakened, and Tessa grabbed onto his shoulders to keep from falling. "Oh Lord," she whispered.

"So sensitive." His hold tightened. "I like that."

"Sir, please."

His free arm went around her waist, pulling her to him. "Trust me, sweetie. I won't let you fall."

Instinctually, she knew that, but what about betrayal? Where the hell was that coming from? Tessa's heart pounded. It must be residual fear from the reporter Wednesday night. Damon had never given her any reason to think he would betray her.

Damon's deep voice broke through her thoughts. "Where are you, sweetie?"

"Sorry, Sir."

"Are you okay?" He let go of her neck and pulled her tighter into his embrace. "We don't have to do this."

"I'm fine, Sir." She gave him a smile. All her thoughts about the reporter could wait. She tucked them away.

"Are you?" Damon stared down at her, his blue eyes filled with concern.

"Yes, Sir." Tessa lifted her chin. "I want to do this, Sir."

He studied her for a moment, then released her. "You have safe words, so use them if needed."

She nodded.

"All right. I want you to undress and get on the bed."

Tessa pulled off her t-shirt as Damon opened the bag. "What's in the bag, Sir?"

"Toys."

She slipped off the rest of her clothes and lay down on the mattress.

"Where are the restraints I gave you?"

Tessa sat up.

"No, stay on the bed. Tell me where they are, and I'll get them."

Heat filled her face.

"Now that's an interesting shade of red, my Tessa."

Oh crap. Why had she put the restraints in that drawer? Her toy drawer. Well, not completely toys. Her vibrator was in there, along with books she didn't share with anyone. And of course, the restraints were there.

"Please, let me get them, Sir."

"Why are you embarrassed?"

Tessa closed her eyes. "I…" She reached down and pulled the comforter over her body.

Damon crossed the room and sat next to her on the bed. "Tessa?" He cupped her cheek.

"Sir…" she started.

"No more sir; this is Damon and Tessa now."

She leaned her cheek into his palm. "I know I shouldn't be embarrassed, but I am."

"Is it because of the restraints or something else?"

"Something else." This didn't make sense. Why did it bother her so much if Damon saw her books? The man had seen her naked, for goodness sake.

"Why did you pull the comforter up?"

Tessa blinked at the question. "I was getting cold."

He tilted his head. "Are you sure? I would have thought you were hot."

"Shit." He was right. She'd been hot, yet she was trying to hide from him. Her fingers curled around the fabric.

"Let it stay." His hand covered hers. "For now. Tell me more about what's in the drawer."

"The restraints and my vibrator," she whispered.

"I don't see you being embarrassed about that. What else?"

Tessa ducked her head. She needed to tell him. Honest, open communication. Taking a shaky breath, she raised her head and looked at him. "Books."

"Books? Why would you be embarrassed about books?"

Tessa didn't answer, and Damon's lips curved up into a smile.

"I'm super curious now. May I?"

"I guess." Fear welled up in her. Would he think her a freak?

Damon stood, walked over to her dresser, and waited. "Bottom drawer."

He opened the drawer, pulled the restraints out and set them on top of the dresser, then pulled out her stack of books. After pushing the drawer closed, he sat on the mattress with the books in hand.

"These look like typical erotic romance books."

"Oh?" In her mind they weren't. Well, not quite true; they were erotic romances, but they went a little further than most.

He set them on the bed and picked the first one up to read the back cover copy. Tessa waited barely breathing.

"Sweetie, I don't see why you were embarrassed."

"May I?" She held her hand out for the book. Damon placed it in her hand. Tessa flipped the pages until she came to the first scene in the book that caused her to squirm every time she read it. "Here, read this."

Damon took the book and began reading. Tessa nibbled on her lower lip, her tummy churning and her heart pounding. He flipped the page and kept reading. Maybe this wouldn't be so bad.

More pages, and then he looked over the top of the book. Their gazes clashed. His were alight with desire. He closed the book and lowered it to the mattress.

"Please explain to me why you're embarrassed by the book?"

Tessa stared at him. "You read part of it." She shifted.

"It's a very sexy, sensual scene."

It was, but… "Damon, he takes total control of her, and she likes it. From the moment they meet, he's all dominant male: downright overbearing and an asshole. He forces her to do his bidding in and out of bed."

"Is that how you see it?"

Tessa hesitated. Damon wasn't upset, he was asking her questions and not jumping to conclusions. "I see it, but what does it say about me that it makes me excited."

"It says you're a woman who is deeply passionate."

"What about the sex scene?" She really couldn't call it

167

a love scene.

"Is that something you want to do?"

"What?" Her thoughts spun around his question.

"Would you like me to tie you up and have my wicked way with you with no input from you? Although I would say the heroine was very vocal." Damon ran his finger over her cheek.

"Yes… No… Oh hell." How did she answer that? Yes, part of her wanted that. For control to be taken from her. Wasn't that part of the D/s relationship?

"Tessa, I know you said you had a mentor, but were you never taught the sub has all the power?"

"Yes, but—" He placed his fingers against her lips.

"No buts. You stop everything with a single word. If this is something you'd like to try, I'm game."

"You don't think I'm a freak?" Maybe she should show him the other scenes that made her hot.

"Sweetie, I don't know who told you that, but you are not a freak. You are a very sensual woman." He slipped his hand to the back of her neck.

Her body heated, and her bones melted. Her upper body went lax.

"This is a sign of complete trust in me. I would never betray that trust." He tightened his hand and released her. "I mean that, Tessa. You say red and everything stops, no matter what."

Tessa swallowed. Damon understood her. "You are planning to restrain me tonight?"

His eyes lit up. "Yes, restraint and toys. I'm not going to tell you what toys."

"And if I beg you to stop."

"You can beg me all you want. Only red will make me stop."

SEDUCE

"Okay," she whispered.

"But first." He picked up another one of the books. "This one is different."

Oh yeah. That was really half erotic romance and half porn. Damon flipped through it. "Ah, I see now. Does my Tessa have kidnap fantasies?"

Her body flushed, and she looked down at her clenched hands.

"Yes, she does." Damon cupped her chin and raised her face to his. "After we've been together for a while, we'll talk and act out your fantasies. I'm willing to make it work for you."

"Damon." His name came out in a plea. No man could be this good or comfortable with kink. At least not in her experience.

"Sweetie, I mean what I say. Nothing I've read so far in these books or about your limits tells me we're not compatible."

Tessa blinked. "You can't be real."

Damon's chuckle became a husky laugh. "Honey, I design adult toys, and I'm a partner in a BDSM club, so of course I'm real. You haven't been around the right men." His eyes darkened with intensity. "Now you are." He gathered up the books and put them away before picking up the restraints. "Lose the cover, sweetie. Time to play."

Tessa blew out a breath and kicked the comforter to the end of the bed and waited.

"That's my girl." He strode to the bed. "Wrists or legs?"

"What?"

He glared at her.

"What do you mean, Sir?"

"Better. Next time you forget, I will give your ass a

169

swat. Do you want your wrists or legs restrained tonight?"

Tessa bit her lip. Having her arms free would mean she could touch him, but she wasn't sure about having her legs restrained. "Wrists, please, Sir."

He nodded. "Arms over your head."

She did as he asked. The sound of him unbuckling the first restraint set her nerves quivering. When he slipped the cuff on her wrist, her pussy clenched. By the time he got to her other wrist, she could barely stay still.

"Are you aroused, my sweet?"

"Very much so, Sir."

"Good. If your arms start to ache or go numb, tell me." He picked up the bag and pulled out his toys, placing them on the bed next to her hip.

Tessa tried to see what the toys were. She noticed one looked like a vibrator, but it was hard to see the other items.

"Now, my sweet. I'm going to play with your breasts and your pussy."

Tessa shifted in her bonds.

"I'll start with something easy." He shifted on the mattress and leaned over her. His lips covered her left breast.

"Ah." Tessa arched into his mouth. His right hand pinched her right nipple, and her clit pulsed. She tugged at her bonds, wanting to curl her fingers into his hair.

He raised his head and let her nipple go with a pop. "There we go, both are hard and needy now." Damon reached down and lifted out a pair of nipple rings.

Her pussy spasmed.

"These are for beginners since you indicated you'd never had nipple rings on before."

"That's correct, Sir." Her breathing was already choppy; how was she going to survive this?

He held up the nipple ring. It wasn't closed on one end, and it had stars on it. "I made these. I only saw your nipples that one night, so let me see if I got the sizing right." He cupped her breast in his palm and slipped the first one on. "How does that feel?"

"Strange, Sir."

"Explain."

"The weight is different. My nipple is throbbing."

"Is it too tight?"

"I don't think so. I feel pressure, but it's not unbearable."

Damon gently touched the ring, and she jumped. "It moves slightly, so it's good for now." He picked up the second ring and applied it. He reached over to her nightstand, and she saw him with his phone.

"Sir?" He wasn't going to take a picture would he?

"Setting a timer." He put his phone back down. "Since you're not unuse to them, I don't want them on more than five minutes."

Tessa blew out a breath.

"So let me continue my exploration." He lowered his head and kissed his way between her breasts and down, laving her belly button with his tongue, then kissing the top of her mound. Her legs shifted. "Ah, sweetie, try to keep still."

Damon rose up and crawled between her legs, widening them with his hands and body as he went. "Such a pretty pussy." He dropped his head and licked her slit.

Her breathing grew choppier. His tongue sent delicious sensations of pleasure from her clit to her nipples. Oh Lord, her nipples were swelling within the rings, and the pressure was causing even more shafts of pleasure to flow through her veins.

"You're wet." Her body flushed. "That pleases me."

Tessa smiled, then groaned as he parted her pussy lips with his fingers. "I think you're ready for toy number two." Their gazes locked.

Something round and hard pressed against her entrance. "Shall I tell you about this little toy I invented for you?"

"Please, Sir." Damn, was that her breathless voice? He did that to her.

"This is a very special vibrator."

Tessa moaned as he withdrew and pushed the vibrator into her pussy.

"It does vibrate, but does so much more." More of the toy filled her. "You see, sweetie. This will vibrate, but it will also twist inside your sweet pussy."

Another moan left her lips as the vibrator was seated, but there was something else. Something against her clit. "Sir, what is against my clit?"

"Oh that." He gave a husky laugh that sent tendrils of desire flowing over her skin. "I'm going to let that be a surprise."

The alarm on his phone went off, and Tessa jumped. "Easy, sweetie." He rocked back on his knees. "Let's get those rings off." Damon rose up over her. "I'll be gentle, but be prepared for the blood rushing back into your nipples."

"Okay, Sir." Tessa closed her eyes.

His fingers removed the first one, then his mouth covered her nipple. What little breath Tessa had in her lungs whooshed out. There wasn't much pain, but her pussy was clenching at the vibrator, and her clit throbbed.

"Good girl. Now the other one."

The second one was as intense as the first one. This

time, her abs tightened, and her toes curled. What the heck? Before she could even process what was happening, she climaxed.

Damon sat up between her legs and had a big grin on his face when she opened her eyes. "Sorry, Sir."

"What are you sorry for?" He tossed the nipple rings onto the bedside table.

"I climaxed, Sir."

He tilted his head as he looked at her. "Sweetie, there's nothing wrong letting go with a climax, unless I tell you otherwise."

"I noticed some Doms don't like it when their sub doesn't ask for permission." Her orgasm had come on so quickly.

"I'm not one of them." He leaned over and brushed a kiss over her lips. "Now, let's see if you can do it again."

The vibrator came to life. Her muscles clenched around the toy. "It feels stronger than a normal vibrator, Sir."

"It should. It's one of my special toys." He turned it up.

"Fuck," Tessa said. The little nub against her clit started moving from side to side. Her clit reacted. She wasn't going to last long with all these sensations. But she wanted Damon inside her, not a toy. She jerked at her bonds. "Please, Sir. I want you to be in me when I come again."

Damon grin widened. "There's no other place I'd rather be." The toy was turned off and removed from her core. The ripping of a wrapper met her ears, and she watched as he sheathed himself before placing his cock at her opening.

"Yes, Sir." She tugged at the restraints, wanting to touch him, to feel his hot skin beneath her fingers.

"Easy, sweetie, you'll hurt yourself." He thrust home.

"Ah." Her neck arched, and her hips flexed up against his.

"You feel so good around me. Tight, wet, and mine."

Tessa couldn't find her voice. His shaft filled her and brought every nerve ending alive. She wrapped her legs around his waist as he began to thrust in and out.

Her lashes slid down as she closed her eyes. Bliss. This was what she needed. A man she trusted, a man she could fall in love with. For a second, everything inside her froze, but then Damon shifted, and she sighed. This was what she was missing in her life.

"You're so beautiful." Damon rained kisses over her face and neck.

"Right back at you." She'd finally found her voice. Her muscles tightened, and tingles began from her arms to her toes. "I'm not going to last much longer."

"Come for me, sweetie." He twisted his hips.

Tessa cried out as another climax flowed over her. Hot waves of pleasure filled her body. And Damon kept thrusting. How much more could she take?

"One more time, sweetie," he said, his words staccato, as if he was having trouble finding the words. Then he thrust one more time as his mouth covered hers.

She screamed as she came again, but this time, Damon stiffened above her, and she felt him pulsing within her.

Her legs fell from their hold around his waist, her body totally spent. Damon rested against her, his tongue tasting the skin of her neck.

"Sir?" She hated to disturb him, but she didn't have a choice.

"Yes, sweetie."

"Ummm, I think my arms have fallen asleep."

"Shit." He sat up and pulled himself from her clinging

body. "Let me get rid of the condom."

Tessa flexed her fingers to get the blood flowing. Damon was back in less than a minute, undoing the restraints. He rubbed her right arm and then her left.

"Are you okay?"

"I'm fine." She flexed her wrists and bent her elbow several times. Her arms encircled his neck. "You are a wonderful man." She smiled then gave him a kiss.

"As long as you're okay." He put his palms on her upper arms.

"Damon, I'm fine. Stop worrying and kiss me."

He smiled and did as she asked.

* * * *

It was after nine before they sat down to have dinner. Damon took over frying the chicken when he noticed how uncomfortable Tessa was with hot oil.

"This came out great," she said. "Thanks to you."

"You needed a little help."

"A lot of help." She sat down her fork. "I don't think I'll ever be a good cook."

"That's what you have me for."

Tessa froze and blinked. She didn't want to make light of his words or take them too seriously. "I do, have you, that is." She hesitated, but she needed to know. "Are we in a relationship?"

Damon grinned. "We've been in one since you came to my house for the picnic."

Her mouth opened and closed. He was right. Okay, awkwardness passed. But another one was coming up. "Will you spend the night?" she asked.

This time, his eyes grew wide. "I would like that, thank you." So darn polite. "I actually have a meeting in town tomorrow morning."

"Oh." She finished off her dinner.

"Yeah. I don't know if you noticed, but the store next to mine is up for sale."

"I didn't know. Are you planning to buy it?"

"Yes. After Wednesday night, I realized the book club needs its own space, and Destiny has been after me to carry more books. I have limited space, so it makes sense."

"That's great."

"You don't sound all that excited." Damon pushed his empty plate away.

"I am, it's—" She broke off. "It's not my place to say."

He reached across the small table and took her hand. "Didn't we confirm we're in a relationship?"

"Yes." She swallowed.

"So tell me what you're thinking, Tessa."

She stared at him. There was honesty in his voice. "Are you, maybe, overextending yourself?"

"Is that what you're worried about?" He stood up, crossed over to her, and pulled her out of her chair into his arms. "I'm fine, sweetheart."

"You might think that, Damon, but all of this is going to take time from you. The club, the adult store, now you want to expand the bookstore, and your toy business picked up a huge contract." She shook her head. "You can't do it all. I've seen too many people in DC overextend themselves and run into issues with their business."

Damon's lips brushed her cheek. "I promise you I'm not overextending. But I thank you for worrying about me. Trust me?"

"Yes." She did. In her heart and in her life.

"Then trust me on this. Now, let's clean up dinner and go back to bed."

Tessa nodded and slipped out of his embrace, but her

worry lay like a lead ball in her stomach.

* * * *

Damon met the real estate agent at ten on Saturday. The storefront had been empty for a while, so there was going to be work to do to clean it up and get things ready, but it made sense. He noted everything that needed to be done and put in an offer.

The real estate agent smiled, telling him she'd talk with the owner. Damon was aware he might have low-balled the offer a bit since the place had only recently been put on the market.

After meeting with the real estate agent, Damon went to the bank and talked with the loan officer. He was assured there would be no issue with a loan to buy the store. Damon also transferred money from his account into the Wicked Sanctuary account.

Once outside the bank, Damon called Max. "Hey Max, an FYI: I transferred money into the club accounts to help with the expansion."

"You didn't have to do that so quickly," Max said.

"I was at the bank anyway, so figured it would be better to do it now than have to worry about it later."

"So you're in town."

"I put in a bid on the store next to mine."

"That's great. Are you going to be able to float a loan to get it?"

Damon laughed. "I'm financially fine. There's no reason to worry."

"Sorry. Habit to worry about my friends."

"Same goes here. Is there anything special on the agenda for the club tonight?"

"Nope. I've got you on DM duty from eight to ten and two to four."

"Late night tonight."

"I also figured we can talk with Colby and Zeke tonight to see if they're willing to accept extra duties."

"That will be good." Damon climbed into his car.

"Are you bringing Tessa with you tonight?"

"Probably. I need something to do between ten and two."

Max laughed. "See you later."

Damon had pulled into his driveway when his cell rang. It was the real estate agent. The owner accepted his bid and wanted to move on selling the place right away. She would send everything through to his email address.

He went into his home office and printed out all the paperwork and began reading, then he called Jordan.

"Hey, Damon."

"Hey. Do you have some time this afternoon?" There was some shuffling noise on the other end.

"How does two work?"

Damon looked at the clock. It was barely eleven-thirty. "That will work."

"What do you want to talk about?"

"I put in an offer on the property, and they accepted the offer."

"That was fast."

"Yeah, I suspect the owners wanted to get out from underneath the property. I have all the stuff from the real estate company."

"Bring everything. Did you get a loan yet?"

"No. I did talk with them, and they said it wouldn't be an issue."

"It shouldn't be. I'll grab one of the paralegals who deals with this stuff in case I miss something."

"Thanks. See you at two." Damon hung up and

gathered up all the printed material into a folder before leaving the house. Sometimes, living out here could be a trial, especially when he had to drive into town a couple times a day, but it was worth it.

On his way back into town, he called Tessa.

"Hello."

"Hello, beautiful. Are you available for lunch?" She was working today.

"Let's see… Oh, who am I kidding? Of course I am." There was laughter in her voice.

"Good. I'm on my way back into town. Meet you at the deli on South Street, or would you rather go to Sweet and Savory?"

"Sweet and Savory, please. I'd rather support Lara than a deli chain."

"You got it. I'll be at the library in about twenty minutes."

"Why don't I meet you at the cafe?"

Damon was about to say no but realized he needed to let Tessa do things on her own. Picking her up and driving her home was habit. He wanted to make sure she was safe. "Okay. See you there."

He hung up with a smile on his face. Today was going quite well.

* * * *

Damon paced outside Sweet and Savory. Where was Tessa? She might have gotten hung up at work, but she would have called if that were the case or at least texted. He fought against trying to call her, but his need to make sure she was okay won out.

Nothing. The phone went directly to voicemail. Where was she? After another ten minutes, he couldn't stand it any longer. He got into his car and started for the library. His

179

phone rang.

"Tessa?" He hadn't even bothered to look at the screen.

"Damon, I'm sorry," she said, her voice soft but tearful.

"Sweetheart, where are you?" He pulled over and parked.

"The emergency room."

Damon's heart sank to his stomach. "Are you okay?"

"I will be. It was a stupid accident."

"We'll talk about it later. I'm on my way." Damon hung up and flipped a U-turn and headed for the local hospital. He finally found a parking spot on the sixth floor of the parking structure, and he ran to the ER.

He tried to be calm as the nurse helped another patient. But his mind was on Tessa.

"How can I help you, sir?" the nurse said.

"My fiancée was brought in here. Tessa Ruthledge." A little white lie, but he wasn't going to let anyone stop him from seeing her.

"Oh yes, sir." She motioned to another nurse. "Would you take this gentleman to room three, please."

"Thank you." Damon followed the other nurse who left him outside of room three. Taking a deep breath, he walked in. Tessa lay on the bed, her face pale and her eyes closed. "Tessa," he whispered.

Her lashes rose. "Hi, Damon." She tried to smile, but it wobbled a bit. "I'm sorry." Her eyes turned glassy.

"Sweetie." He went to her side, and took her hand. "What happened?"

"A silly accident." She wiped her tears with the hand that didn't have an IV in it. "I was coming out of the library and somehow slipped on the last stair."

"Those stairs are concrete."

"Yep." She started to nod and winced. "I've got a bruised tailbone for sure. The doctor is checking on the other tests to make sure I don't have a concussion."

"You hit your head?" His hand tightened on hers.

"Yeah. I didn't pass out or anything. I mainly landed on my ass. Good thing I have lots of padding back there."

"Don't joke." Damon frowned at her. He could have lost her to a stupid accident. His heart clenched.

"Please don't worry. I'll be fine."

"Of course you will." He fought back the urge to gather her up into his arms and never let go. As she said, it was an accident. But he couldn't stop the feeling of dread in his stomach.

The curtain was pushed back, and an older gentleman in a white jacket came strolling in. "Hello. I'm Dr. Newman," he said, holding out his hand.

"Damon Kline, Tessa's fiancé."

"Very good. X-rays are clean. I'm not seeing any concussion related symptoms, and her imaging studies are all clear."

"She winced when she tried to nod," Damon said.

"Oh." The doctor walked over to the bed, and Damon backed away. "Does it hurt?"

"A little bit." Tessa said. "A little bit of a headache and a little ache in the neck."

The doctor had Tessa lean forward and he felt around her neck.

"There's no question that you're going to have some soreness in your neck and back, and some bruising in your buttocks and hip, all from your fall. Ice to keep the swelling down and warm compresses to help with muscle spasm. Tylenol or ibuprofen for pain. You're going to feel rough around the edges for the next three or four days. If you

181

experience any dizziness, nausea, vomiting, or headache not helped by the ibuprofen or Tylenol, come back right away or call your primary care doc. The nurse will be in with your discharge papers and to remove the IV." He went over to the computer and typed in a few things.

"Thank you," Tessa said.

"Thank you, Doctor," Damon commented. The doctor nodded and left the room. Damon took her hand again.

"I'm sorry. You don't need to wait here with me."

"Nonsense. What kind of fiancé would I be if I didn't?"

"Damon, we're not engaged."

"Not yet."

Tessa sighed and closed her eyes. Damon stood there holding her hand as she rested. The adrenaline rush was leaving him, but he wasn't going to leave her alone. Not now. Not ever.

* * * *

"Damon, I'm fine. Go to work at the club," Tessa said as she lay her head back on the soft sofa pillows. She was getting frustrated. Yes, her head hurt a little bit, but that was it, and they still hadn't discussed his fiancé comment.

"Doctor said you shouldn't be alone."

"He did not. He said to watch out for signs of a concussion, but nothing showed up on any of the tests. I took some ibuprofen, and my head barely hurts."

"I'm going to call Max and see if he can cover for me."

"No, you won't." Tessa had had enough. "You have a responsibility to Max and Jordan, for that matter. I know you don't take that lightly."

"I don't." He crossed his arms over his chest and looked down at her where she lay on the sofa. His sofa. The damn man refused to take her home, had carried her into the house, and plunked her down with an admonition to stay put.

"Then go."

"Not going to happen."

"Damn stubborn man." She picked up her cell phone, which luckily had survived her fall. "Hey, Sierra. Any chance I can hang out with you at your place tonight?"

"Sure. What's going on?"

"I'll explain when I get there. Thanks." She hit the off button and looked up at Damon. "There. Settled. I'll stay with Sierra, and you can work."

Damon's scoff carried a hint of amusement. "Stubborn woman."

"I could say the same about you."

"Fine." He threw his hands up. "But you will rest. No running around with Sierra. No coming over to the club. You will behave yourself."

"Yes, oh lord and master."

"Don't you forget it." Damon stomped off, and Tessa couldn't help grinning. She'd won one battle, but there was still a war to be fought.

* * * *

"I don't think I've ever seen Damon so worried before," Sierra said after Damon left.

"The man is paranoid." Tessa adjusted her position on the sofa. "I really don't need to lie here like an invalid."

"I'm not about to cross a Dom when he's in the mood Damon is in." Sierra sat in the overstuffed chair. "What would you like to watch?" She started to scroll through the apps on the TV.

"Wait a second. Is this the Sierra who refused to give up her DVD collection in favor of using a smart TV and streaming?" Tessa gaped at her friend.

Sierra ducked her head. "That's what happens when

you marry an IT guy."

Tessa laughed. They settled on a musical and sat back to watch.

* * * *

Damon was in a foul mood as he walked the club floor. Tessa had outwitted him on this, but he'd made it clear to both Tessa and Sierra that Tessa was to rest and not so much as lift a finger to do anything.

Tessa had stuck her tongue out at him, and he'd showed her a better way to use her tongue. Such a way that he left her breathless and flushed.

"Okay?" Max asked.

"Better. How are the girls?"

"Tired of being checked up on. Do you want me to take the two to four shift?"

"No. You do enough as it is. Tessa is safe at your house. She'll fall asleep, and I can carry her out to the car."

"She didn't look thrilled that you were carting her around when you brought her into the house," Max said.

"She'll learn." Damon was insistent about making sure Tessa was safe. He didn't want her falling again. Not on his watch.

"Who will learn?" Jordan asked coming up to them.

"Tessa. Where's Crystal?" Damon asked.

"She decided to spend time with Tessa and Sierra," Jordan said.

"Good." That made Damon happy. Tessa would be comforted by her friends.

"I don't know. You know those three can get into trouble," Jordan said.

"Sierra is under strict rules," Max said.

"When has that ever stopped her?" Jordan commented.

Damon swore. "Maybe I should go check on them."

"Hey." Jordan touched his arm. "I just left there. They're fine. Sierra was whipping up a bowl of popcorn, and they were going to watch a movie."

Damon nodded. It was nine o'clock; he was off shift in an hour, and he could go check on them.

"Look, you take my midnight to two shift, and I'll take the two to four shift," Jordan offered.

"You've had a long week," Damon said. "Sorry I missed our meeting this afternoon."

"Tessa comes first. I'll come out to your house tomorrow and look over the paperwork. As for my long week, not a big deal."

"I'm fine. I'm sure Tessa will fall asleep soon, so I'll check on her before I start my shift. And Max will be there in case she needs anything." He almost hated letting Max take care of Tessa, but in this case, it was a necessity. As Tessa had reminded him, he'd made a commitment, and he took that seriously.

"Okay. When do you meet with the bank?" Jordan asked.

"I set up an appointment for Monday morning. The bank manager has already assured me that the loan will be processed quickly so I can get moving on the store." There was a lot to do. Good thing he could handle the details from home tomorrow so he could keep an eye on Tessa.

"Have you talked to Zeke yet?" Max asked.

"I left him a message, figured we'd catch up on Monday. I thought he and Colby were going to be here tonight?"

"Apparently not, but it's okay. I'll set up a meeting for all of us next week. Are you guys available Tuesday evening?" Max asked.

"I should be," Jordan said.

"Sure." By then, Tessa would be better.

"All right. We'll talk to them then about becoming DMs for us." Max walked away.

"Better make my rounds," Damon said, and he left Jordan.

* * * *

"Damon, you're being stubborn as a mule on a cold day." Tessa crossed her arms over her chest. It was Sunday afternoon, and he had refused to take her home. Jordan had come and gone, and Damon was still being fussy.

"You need to rest."

"That's all I've done practically all weekend. I'm not dizzy or nauseous. No headaches since yesterday evening. I'm fine."

"It doesn't mean you can't fall again."

Tessa took a deep breath and closed her eyes, before opening them. "Damon, it was a freak accident. You need to understand that."

"Still."

"What's going on? This overprotective male persona is getting old fast."

"I want you to be safe." His voice was strained.

Tessa put her hand on his tense arm. "It's more than that. What has you so worried?" It was more than her accident. There was something else there.

"If you want to go home, I can't stop you." He shook off her touch.

"You can. You're my ride."

He stared at her. Tessa stepped up to him and put her arms around his waist and hugged him. "Damon, I'm fine. I swear it. Please, talk to me." She didn't want him worrying about her.

He stood in her embrace, stiff, then his arms went

around her, and his muscles relaxed. "Remember I told you I lost my parents the day after my college graduation?"

"Yes."

"An accident took them too."

"The plane accident." She remembered his story.

"Yes. I don't want to lose you to an accident too. To anything."

"Oh, Damon." She tightened her hold on him. "These things happen; we can't always predict them. But I promise to be more careful. Can you accept that?"

"For now," he said softly.

Tessa would take it. "So will you drive me home, please? I need to get ready for work tomorrow."

"Before I do that, there is something you should see." He stepped out of her embrace and picked up the morning paper. She'd been surprised that he still received a physical newspaper. "This came out today." He handed her a folded over page.

Tessa took it and looked down. Her heart dropped. "Oh crap." She quickly read the article the reporter had written about them at the coffee shop along with a grainy picture of them. How many people had seen this picture? Would it get back to DC? It shouldn't. Her stomach turned over.

"It's pure gossip and innuendo."

"Yes." What could she do about it? Nothing. The odds of someone who knew her and showing it to her father were slim to none.

"Are you upset?"

"A little," she lied. "But I'm sure this will all blow over." She hoped.

By Tuesday night, Tessa wasn't so sure. Damn it, somehow the picture had been brought to her father's attention.

"Dad, it's nothing."

"Who is this man with his arm around you?" her father demanded.

"He's a friend, like the others in the picture are friends." Oh, but he was so much more. Damon meant a lot to her, and they were in a relationship, but she wasn't going to tell her father that. "Really, Dad," she continued as he kept ranting. "It was a casual date, and I probably won't see him again."

She hated lying, but she didn't want her father blowing any more of a gasket than he already was.

"Well, it's a good thing your brother will be out there next week to check up on you."

Damn, she'd forgotten that. "I don't need to be checked up on. I'm fine."

"Be nice to your brother, and no more pictures in the paper." The line went dead.

Tessa huffed and flopped down on her sofa. Ouch. Damn it. Bruised tailbone, remember. How was she going to explain to Damon why she didn't want to be seen in public with him?

* * * *

Damon had a spring in his step as he walked into Wicked Sanctuary Friday afternoon. They hadn't been able to get together with Zeke and Colby until today, but that was okay. After going to the bank on Monday, and signing all the paperwork, progress was being made on buying the building next door.

The real estate agent was rushing everything through. The owners were happy to have a buyer, and Damon was happy to get the building as soon as possible. He walked down the hall to the classroom. Tessa would meet him there later.

Tessa. She'd been very quiet this week. She didn't mind eating dinner at her apartment or his place. But she wouldn't meet him for lunch. He'd been in town quite a bit, and each time, she had an excuse. He planned on asking her about it this weekend.

Max and Jordan were already in the room. "Zeke and Colby going to make it?"

"Yeah," Max said. "I told them six to give us time to chat."

"Has something happened?" Damon asked taking a seat.

"No. I wanted you to know Zeke hired an architect to draw up plans for the club. I'll be meeting with the architect next week, and I wasn't sure if you two wanted to be involved."

"I'm fine with you handling it," Jordan said.

"Me too. I've got enough on my plate."

"So I hear. Congrats on buying the new storefront," Max said.

"How did you know?" Damon shook his head.

"You know our women share everything," Jordan said.

"Maybe I should talk to one of them about Tessa," Damon mused.

"What's going on? Tessa still mad at you for last weekend?" Max asked.

"No, she got over my protectiveness." Could he talk to his friends about this? Why not? "She's been very quiet this week. Won't go to lunch with me but no problem with dinner at her place or mine."

"She's coming tonight, right? I reserved the bondage chair for you at nine," Max said.

"She'll be here. I'm wondering why it feels like she's pulling back."

Max looked up. "We'll talk more later."

Zeke and Colby walked in. "Come sit down," Max said. "The reason I asked you here today is that we were wondering if you two would like to be dungeon monitors in the club."

"What would it entail?" Colby asked.

"I know what a DM is, but what exactly do you want us to do?" Zeke asked.

"It would be a paid position," Max said.

Damon nodded. He, Max, and Jordan had covered this in the earlier meeting.

"Ideally, we'd like one of you available from eight to midnight on Friday and Saturday nights."

"Two of us would take the midnight to four shift," Damon added.

"We're looking at a hundred-fifty each weekend you work," Max said.

Colby leaned back in his chair. "I don't know about Zeke, but I'd rather have my yearly membership comped."

"I like that idea," Zeke said.

"So you two are on board?" Jordan asked.

"Hell, yeah," Colby said.

"What do we need to sign? And when do we start?" Zeke asked.

Jordan laughed. "Give me time to create a new contract stating you're working for membership fees."

"If you both could come here next Thursday night, we can go over exactly what we need from both of you," Max said.

"Not a problem. We can play when we're not working, right?" Colby asked.

"Yes, you're not restricted in that manner." Max grinned.

"All right." Zeke stood. "We have a deal." He held out his hand. They all shook.

"I got your message, Damon," Zeke said. "Sorry. It's been crazy at work."

"No problem. I bought the store next to mine. I wanted you to come over and look at what needs to be done," Damon said.

"Do you have the keys?"

"Not yet."

"Once you get them, call me, and we'll set up a time." Zeke waved as he walked out of the room.

"That reminds me. I'll have the prototype for the wristbands you wanted ready by next week," Colby announced and followed Zeke out the door.

"That went well," Max said.

"It did, but you know, once we expand, we're going to need more help," Damon said.

"I do. I already have ideas, but those are for another day. Let's go get ready for our women."

* * * *

Tessa walked into the club with a heavy heart. Not because she was going to play with Damon tonight, but because her brother was due to arrive Monday. She so didn't want to deal with him.

"Hey, why the sad face?" Crystal asked as Tessa walked into the women's room.

"Sorry, thinking about a problem." While her friends knew about her father being a politician, they didn't know the whole story. She forced herself to smile. Tessa really didn't want anything to intrude on her time with Damon tonight. This would be their last weekend together until her brother left. She didn't plan on having her brother meet Damon, but anything could happen. Maybe she should tell

Damon about her brother's visit. Ugh, why couldn't she get this figured out.

She slipped off her coat and removed the gloves from her bag. She pulled them on, smoothed her hands down over the corset and turned to face her friends.

"Holy shit," Sierra exclaimed.

"Too much?" She stared at her friend. The outfit was one of her favorites, and she wanted Damon to be proud of her in the club tonight.

"I bet Damon strips those gloves off the second you get into the scene," Crystal said. The black evening gloves extended up her arms.

"Turn around," Sierra commanded.

Tessa did a little spin, enjoying the way the skirt flared.

"That's perfect. I love how the skirt is sewn into the corset," Sierra said.

"The red and black is going to drive Damon crazy," Crystal said.

Tessa smiled. She hoped so. This was a daring outfit for her. Well, sort of. The corset itself barely covered her breasts but ended right below them, pushing her boobs up.

"Come on. I want to watch our Doms' reactions before everyone gets here." Sierra took her arm.

The three made their way into the club. The music was already on. Damon, Max, and Jordan were standing near the bar. Tessa took a deep breath and started toward them.

Damon saw her first, and his mouth dropped open.

* * * *

Damon caught movement from the corner of his eye and turned. He couldn't stop himself from gaping.

Tessa was a vision. The black corset had red stripes going through it. The corset ended below her breasts, pushing them up until they threatened to spill out of the black satin bra she wore.

The black skirt fell below her ass and was edged with a red trimmed ruffle. Her legs and feet were encased in black heels. And the black satin gloves. His skin itched to feel that satin against his skin.

Damon was barely aware of Max and Jordan turning as he made his way to Tessa. "You look fantastic," he said, taking those gloved hands in his. Who knew gloves could be so sexy?

"You like?"

"I love the outfit." Damon leaned forward. "You in it is sexy as hell. You'll be even sexier out of it," he whispered.

Tessa flushed.

"Tessa, dear, you are a vision of loveliness," Max said.

"Sexy as hell," Jordan commented.

"Down, boys," Sierra said.

The men laughed. Damon drew Tessa to the side. "Are you ready for our scene tonight?"

"Yes." Her voice had a little tremble to it.

"Everything okay?"

"Just nervous."

"I understand. I've got the first hour on DM duty. Jordan will take over so we can scene, then I'll pick up at midnight so Crystal and Jordan can play."

"What about Sierra and Max?"

"Oh, they'll play too." Damon smiled. It was the first night all three of them were going to play in the club together.

Later, after Damon's duty, Tessa's breath caught in her throat when Damon walked into the green area. He held out his hand to her. Taking a deep breath, she allowed him to pull her to her feet.

"Tonight we're going to play in the bondage area," he

193

said.

"Yes, Sir." They'd talked about it on the phone the other night. She was as prepared as she could be.

Damon's bag already sat on the stage with the bondage chair. Tessa swallowed. Okay, she hadn't expected that. He helped her up on the stage.

"All right, my sweet. Can we get rid of the corset?"

She hesitated, and Damon stepped up to her and cupped her cheeks.

"What do you have on underneath?"

"A thong and, of course, the bra, as you can see, Sir."

"Then why the hesitation."

"The corset and skirt are one piece, Sir."

"I see. Are you okay being revealed?"

"Yes, Sir." She wasn't feeding him a line. She reached for the zipper hidden in the side of the corset.

"Let me." Damon brushed her hands away. A small tremor swept through her body as his fingers guided the zipper down. He peeled the corset away, then swept it and the skirt down her body. "Hands on my shoulders, then step out of your clothing."

Tessa did as he asked. Now she was in high-heeled black shoes, a thong, bra, and gloves.

"How the hell did I get so lucky?" Damon muttered after he put her corset and skirt on the straight-back chair.

His hands closed over her shoulders. "Let's get you into the bondage chair."

She swallowed as he guided her over. He'd said bondage but never mentioned the chair. Sneaky man. There was a cushion on the seat and against the back.

"I haven't forgotten you bruised your tailbone," Damon whispered in her ear.

Heat filled her as she sat down on the wooden

contraption, the cushions protecting her. It was like any other chair, but something told her it wasn't a normal chair.

"As we discussed, if your arms or legs go numb, you tell me right away."

"Yes, Sir." He hadn't been happy that night in her apartment when she didn't tell him the second it happened, but she wasn't going to interrupt him mid stroke to undo the restraints. He'd forgiven her when she promised not to let it happen again.

He adjusted the arms on the chair. "I'm going to keep these pretty level so your arms don't go to sleep." He patted the armrests.

Tessa placed her arms where Damon directed, and he started buckling the restraints over her wrists and upper arms.

"Is this a front clasping bra?"

"Yes, Sir. As you requested." It had taken her several days to find one without underwires.

"Good. Now for your legs."

The chair split between her legs. Wait a second? She hadn't noticed that. There was now enough room for Damon to restrain her upper thighs and ankles.

"I forgot to ask before I did your legs. I'm going to cut the thong off, so I hope it's not your favorite."

"No, Sir. I have others." Her heart sped up at his words. She was going to be pretty much fully nude for this scene. Excitement with a tiny bit of apprehension filled her. But she trusted Damon. He wouldn't betray her.

"Good. I'm going to use my toys."

Tessa groaned, and he grinned at her.

"Don't worry; I have new toys for tonight."

"That's what I'm afraid of, Sir." He was close enough; she shifted her head forward and gave him a kiss.

195

"Cheeky." Damon tweaked her nipple and backed away.

Tessa took a deep breath, closed her eyes, and let her other senses take over. Her muscles relaxed. She was aware people were starting to gather around.

A warm earthy scent tickled her nose. Damon. She'd know him anywhere. "Do you want a blindfold?"

"No, Sir. I want to be able to see what you're doing to me." Later, she'd open her eyes and watch, but right now, she wanted to absorb his touch, his words.

The sound of her bra being snapped open was loud to her ears. "Your breasts are perfect, just like you." His fingers played with her nipples. "Pale globes, yet your nipples turn a deep pink when I play with them and deepen to a rose color as I pinch and use clamps on them."

Tessa tried to shift her hips, but she was restrained too well. His words made her pussy clench with need.

"Let's start with some clamps and work our way from there." Damon's warm breath caressed her skin as he played with her nipples. "I'm using tweezer clamps, as we discussed. I won't keep them on for long."

A pinch and the first one was attached, then the second one. Tessa waited and moaned as Damon tightened them. "Yellow, Sir." It took her a few minutes to catch her breath. The clamps weren't too tight but tight enough.

"Good girl." Damon brushed a kiss over her lips, then he was gone.

Tessa took several deep breaths, feeling the clamps move with her breathing. The crowd murmured as Damon's heat reached her.

"Time for the thong to go." Cool metal touched her hip, followed by a slight tightening of the fabric before it fell away. When he moved to her other hip, all she felt was the coolness of the scissors. "I'm going to pull the fabric out from under you."

Bracing her feet on the floor, Tessa lifted her butt up to help. Not that there was much leeway the way she was restrained, but the change of position gave him a little bit of room to remove the fabric.

"Now, my sweet." His hands were on her inner thighs, and he pushed. The legs of the chair moved outward along with her bound legs.

Oh brother. The air caressed her pussy as she was exposed. Tessa bit her lower lip as she tried to catch her breath. He did say he was going to play with her.

"Your body is flushed. Is it from excitement or embarrassment?"

"Both, Sir." Her eyes were still closed. Did she dare open them to see if her friends were watching? No, she couldn't think about that, or she'd be calling out her safe word. They were all adults, and nudity was a natural thing, but she still couldn't look.

"There's nothing to be embarrassed about."

His voice was now next to her ear. He'd moved, and she hadn't noticed. Oh damn, that meant everyone could see her without obstruction. Her breath hiccupped.

"Easy." His voice was soft. "It's just you and me. I love how flushed you are with excitement. Your nipples are hard little pebbles. I bet your clit is pulsing."

"Yes, Sir." It was, and her muscles were clenching and unclenching.

"Very good." His voice dropped to a deeper, huskier tone.

Oh damn. Her pussy moistened, and her bones weakened. That Dom voice. It got to her every time.

"I'm going to tease you and bring you to climax."

197

"Yes, Sir." Her words were soft and dreamy. Tessa shivered when Damon moved away, but she refused to open her eyes to see what he was doing. No, this is where she wanted to be. To allow him to take control.

Damon's fingers trailing over her arm made her shiver. "Easy, my darling." His heat was between her legs now. Calling out to her. She tried to shift her hips, but couldn't move. Damn him.

His chuckle reached her ears. "Don't worry. I'll make sure you are satisfied."

Tessa tried to slow her breathing down, but it was difficult. Her body had other ideas. Her skin felt tight, as if every nerve was exposed.

"Lift your ass like you did before, sweetheart."

Concentrating, she did as he asked. Something cool and flat slipped beneath her. What was he up to?

"I didn't want to repeat myself with my toys. This is a brand new one I finished developing early this week." He deepened his tone enough to keep her relaxed and on the edge of bliss. "You see," he continued as his fingers parted her pussy lips. "I wanted something that would hold my toy in place while I played with other parts of your body."

"You are a devious man, Sir."

Damon laughed. He rubbed his finger over her clit until it was hard and wanting. "So now I'm going to place my toy right here." A round cool metal was placed against her clit.

Wait a second. His fingers were gone, yet the toy was pressed solidly against her clit. Oh, this was going to be interesting.

"Now, sweetheart." His voice was next to her ear. "Let's have some fun."

The toy began to vibrate against her clit. Okay, he'd

198

put a bullet against her clit, not a biggie.

"Time." Jordan's voice reached her ears. Time for what?

"Let's get these clamps off of you."

Crap. Once he removed them, blood would rush back to her nipples, and while it was a little painful, it was more pleasure. Would he be upset if she climaxed too early?

"Don't worry. I have a plan," he whispered. She felt the first clamp drop against her skin, yet her nipple was still being pinched. Damon was pinching it and ever so slowly releasing the pressure.

Torturous release. There was no pain, only pleasure. When he finished with the clamps, he turned the bullet up.

Her mouth opened on a moan, and he turned it up again. What? She tugged at her legs. That bullet was doing something more than vibrating.

"What is that, Sir?" She couldn't get enough air. Her skin was ultra-sensitive. If she didn't know better she would think there was electricity running through her veins.

"That my love"—he paused, and the vibration increased along with the bullet—"is what makes this special."

Tessa tried to concentrate on the toy. What was it doing? Yes, the vibrations were there, but it was like…someone was licking her clit.

"Ahhh." The noise escaped from her lips as he turned the toy up, and the tongue moved faster. She wanted to shift her hips so badly, to hit that right spot that would send her over, but she couldn't move.

The vibrations increased. Tessa's legs shook. She was right there. A little bit more and she'd go over.

"That's it, sweetie." Damon's husky Dom voice invaded her being. "Let it go. I'm here to catch you."

199

"Yes," she cried out as the toy sped up, the tongue lashing her clit. Her head thrashed against the padded back, and the vibrations increased yet again. She fought her body's reaction.

Every nerve tingled with electricity, and her pussy clenched tighter and tighter. The vibrations increased again. Damn, how many settings did that thing have?

Panting, Tessa fought each tingle, each shaft of pleasure.

"Now, sweetheart. Come for me."

His voice and the toy pushed her over the edge. Tessa cried out, and her body spasmed. The chair shook with the force of her climax. Her head fell forward, and she knew nothing more.

* * * *

Damon knew the instant Tessa fainted. Her body went limp as her climax continued.

"Sweet, sweet, Tessa." He kissed her cheek before turning his toy off.

The audience sighed, causing Damon to smile. He quickly removed the toy and the holder.

"Tessa, honey." He made sure to keep his voice level. There was no response. Damon undid the restraints on her legs, then looked around. Max stood near the stage. "Max, some help please."

His friend was there in an instant. "What do you need?"

"I'm going to undo this arm. When I tell you, would you undo her other one?" Max nodded. Damon unfastened her left arm. It fell limply over his shoulder. Damon slipped his left arm around her waist. "Now, Max."

Tessa slumped against him. She was out of it. Totally and completely out. "Can you grab me the blanket, please?"

200

Max picked up the blanket and handed it to Damon. "Go to the aftercare area. I can clean up for you."

"Thank you." He had wonderful friends. Damon picked Tessa up in his arms and made his way to one of the sofas in the aftercare area. Her head lulled against his shoulder when he sat down, but a smile curved her lips.

"Tessa, sweetie," he said, trying to pull her back to him.

"Just a few more minutes. I'm enjoying myself."

"All right."

* * * *

Damon held Tessa in his arms for a half an hour before she spoke again. She was all soft and relaxed. "I'm not sure I'll ever move again," she said softly.

He smiled at her. "Enjoyed that, did you?"

"You and your damn toys. I think I'm still having mini orgasms." Damon chuckled. "Don't laugh, you sex fiend." Her fist thumped his chest.

He couldn't hide his happiness. Seeing his friends laughing, talking, and cuddling with their women, he wanted what they had. Damon was well on his way with Tessa. He gazed down at her.

Oh yes, he was falling for her. He wanted to be with her all the time. It was too early to tell her, but he would soon.

CHAPTER ELEVEN

Tessa glanced at the text from her brother. His plane had landed, and he was getting a car to drive to her house, which gave her about two hours before he'd arrive. She sighed.

"Damon, I need to go home." It wasn't unusual for a Sunday afternoon, and she did have to work tomorrow.

"Okay." He pulled her into his arms. "Dinner tomorrow night?"

"I'm not sure." She pulled back.

Damon frowned. "What's going on, Tessa?"

"What?" She shook her head. "I'm sorry. I'm distracted." She sighed again. How would Damon take to knowing about her brother's visit? Heck, that wasn't as worrisome as meeting her brother. "My brother is coming to town."

"So that means you can't see me?" His voice grew deeper.

"Yes and no." She cupped his cheek. "I don't want to pull you into my family politics. That's all."

He studied her, and Tessa held his gaze. She was falling for Damon. He was becoming more important to her than anyone. She had no clue what her brother wanted, but she didn't want Damon caught in the middle.

"I don't even know how long my brother is staying. Maybe later in the week?" God, she hated telling his half-truths. But she couldn't risk it right now. What if her brother pulled a fast one? In her heart, she knew Damon wouldn't betray her, but she didn't trust her brother.

His eyes lightened. "All right." He brushed his lips over hers. "Call me."

"Always." She'd gotten used to calling him when she got home from his house and from work. Damon was protective and part of her liked that. "You're going to be busy with the new store. You get the keys tomorrow, right?" The real estate agent had called him today. He'd sign the closing papers tomorrow.

"True."

Tessa slipped from his arms and picked up her bag. "See you soon." She walked to her car and drove away, watching Damon fade in the mirror. Her heart crumpled. This was going to be a long week.

* * * *

"Come on, Tessa. I want to meet this man my sister is dating," her brother, Allen, said on Wednesday evening.

"Allen, I told Dad it's just something casual."

"Right, that's why you call him every evening when you get home."

Tessa's cheeks turned pink. Damn it, she'd hoped he hadn't noticed that. She always made the phone call from her bedroom.

"I knew it." Her brother crowed. "Come on, Tessa, what is one little dinner going to hurt?"

"If I do this, there are going to be some ground rules."

"Oh?" Her brother studied her.

"Yes. You will behave yourself and not ask any political questions."

"I can do that."

"No big brother crap." She held up her hand when he opened his mouth. "No asking what his plans are with me or anything like that. Got it?"

"I promise."

"Keep your promise." Tessa walked away. She picked up her cell and dialed Damon's number.

"Hey, sweetie. I've missed you."

Damon's voice was like a balm to her heart. "Me too. Are you free for dinner tomorrow night?" It was Thursday, and it was quite possible he'd be needed at the club.

"I am. So I get to meet your brother?"

"Yes." She sighed. "Allen wants to meet you. I've already warned him not to do any big brother crap."

"I thought he was younger."

"He is, but that doesn't stop him."

Damon laughed, and Tessa grinned. She missed him so much. The way they'd talk over dinner, debate local news, and just be together.

"Where shall I meet you?"

"I don't have a clue." Most the places her brother would approve of would take reservations at least a week ahead.

"What about the Pleasant Valley Steakhouse?" Damon asked.

"I thought about that, but it's hard to get a reservation. I guess I could call and see if they've had a cancellation."

"Let me call for you. I can get us a table."

"Damon, don't go to any trouble." She was tempted to let him take care of it.

"Give me fifteen minutes and I'll call you back." The line went dead, and Tessa shook her head.

It didn't even take him that long. He called her back in five minutes. "Got it."

"I want to know your trick."

"It's all in who you know. Tomorrow at seven."

"Perfect. Thank you, Damon. I can't wait to see you."

"Me either. Are PDAs allowed?"

204

"PDA?"

"Public displays of affection."

She laughed. Why did her mind think something different? "PG versions, yes."

"Oh dear, then I guess I better leave the vibrating bullet at home."

There was laughter in his voice, and she was happy. Things had been a little cool between them since Sunday. She was responsible for that.

"Until tomorrow," she said softly.

"Until them, my love."

Tessa froze. He'd said, "my love". She shook her head. They were just words; Damon didn't mean them in the way she was taking them. They hadn't known each other long enough. Who was she kidding? She was falling for Damon. Hard and fast. Time didn't mean anything. Hadn't she learned that from her father and her ex?

Not now. She reminded herself. Once her brother was gone, maybe she could analyze these feelings, but not now.

"We have reservations at seven tomorrow night at the Pleasant Valley Steakhouse," she told her brother.

"Perfect. My last meeting is at four; it will give me time to get back here and shower. I can't wait to meet this man you're dating."

Tessa rolled her eyes. No matter what she said, he wasn't listening to her.

* * * *

Tessa ran her hands down her dress as she and her brother walked into the restaurant the next night. Why was she so nervous about Allen and Damon meeting? Her stomach churned. She didn't fully trust her brother.

"Good evening, welcome to the Pleasant Valley Steakhouse. Do you have a reservation?" the hostess asked.

"We're meeting Damon Kline," Tessa said.

"Oh yes, please follow me."

Allen raised his eyebrows but indicated Tessa should precede him. Damon stood when he saw them approaching. This time, they had a table near the front of the restaurant.

"Tessa." Damon took her hands in his and kissed her cheek.

"Damon." Her heart lightened at seeing him. Talking to him on the phone and texting had been good, but there was nothing better than seeing him in person.

Allen clearing his throat made her turn. "Damon, this is my brother, Allen. Allen, Damon Kline, a friend." She put an emphasis on friend. Damon gave her a pointed look, and Tessa knew they'd be discussing the 'friend' comment later. Right now, the last thing she needed was her brother poking into her love life.

Allen held his hand out. "Mr. Kline."

"Damon, please." They shook hands, and Damon held out a chair for her.

The waiter came right over, took their drink orders, and disappeared.

"This looks good," Allen said as he looked over the menu.

"Their food is excellent." She glanced at Damon and grinned.

The waiter returned with their drinks and asked if they were ready. They were, so they all ordered.

"So, Damon, what do you do?" Allen asked.

Tessa almost choked on her iced tea at the question.

"I'm an engineer."

Whew! Neutral answer. She should have clued Damon in. Not that she thought he'd say anything wrong. Maybe this wasn't such a good idea. Damon was cool as a cucumber, but Tessa was a basket case.

"Nice. Where did you go to school?" Allen stared at Damon.

"MIT." Damon slipped his hand to Tessa's leg and squeezed.

Allen nodded. "So how long have you been dating my sister?"

"Allen!" Tessa sputtered. "We talked about this."

"It's a fair question," Allen said. "I have a right to know about my sister's love life."

"I'm going to disagree with you there," Damon said in that firm voice of his. "What is between Tessa and me remains between us."

"Really?" Allen raised his eyebrows. "And that picture in the gossip column?"

Tessa groaned. Why didn't the floor open up and swallow her? She should have known better.

"Unfortunate happenstance. We were out with friends when that reporter intruded. It was coffee with friends." While Damon kept his tone level, Tessa heard the thread of annoyance.

"I explained this, Allen." Movement caught her eye, and Tessa turned her head. What the hell was a photographer doing here?

Allen turned and smiled as the picture was taken.

"Thank you, sir," the man said and scurried away.

Tessa's hands closed into fists. "You set that up." Why did she think she could trust her brother? Allen knew she wanted to stay out of the limelight and not be connected to her political family, yet he did this anyway.

"Of course. Congressional candidate out to dinner with his sister and her beau." Allen grinned.

"I'm so sorry, Mr. Kline," the maître d' said as he

rushed to the table.

"Not your fault, Barry." Damon's tone was cool, not quite icy, and his demeanor morphed from cordial to controlled dominance. "I'll bring a bottle of your favorite wine."

"No need. It's fine." Damon glared at her brother as Barry left. "Why did you feel the need to embarrass your sister?"

"How did I embarrass her? It was just a picture."

Damon stiffened next to her. Anger filled her own veins, but she couldn't lose it in the restaurant. Too many eyes. Too many phones, pictures to be taken. She never should have agreed to this.

"I want to leave." She stood up, and Damon did the same.

"Come on, Tessa. I'm in the mood for a good steak," Allen cajoled.

Tessa's mouth dropped open. "I don't know what happened to you, Allen. I would say too much time with Dad, but somehow I don't think that's it." She broke off when another man approached the table.

"Allen," the man said.

"Representative Hopper." Allen rose to his feet, and they shook hands.

"Please, don't let me interrupt," Hopper said.

"We were about leaving," Tessa said as she fought to keep the anger out of her voice.

"Tessa," Allen said. "This is my sister, Tessa, and her friend, Damon Kline. This is Representative Hopper. I met with him this afternoon."

Tessa ground her teeth together. She wouldn't make a scene no matter how much she wanted to. "If you'll excuse me." She didn't wait for an answer. She slipped by Damon and walked away with her head held high.

* * * *

Damon watched Tessa stride away. His first need was to go after her, but he had something to take care of first. His anger rose. What the hell was wrong with her brother?

"Are you going to sit back down, Damon?" Allen asked.

"No." Damon took a breath. "If this is how you treat your sister, then you don't deserve her."

Allen bristled. "How I treat my sister is none of your business."

"It is my business. Do this to her again, and I'll have your ass. Good evening." Damon walked off, pleased to see both Allen and Hopper standing there with shocked faces.

Damon reached the parking lot and looked for Tessa. She was standing next to her vehicle. "Tessa," he said softly when he approached.

"I can't drive," she said, turning to him, her body shaking.

While her face was composed, there were tears in her eyes.

"No, you can't." Damon fished his phone out of his pocket. "Hey, Jordan, can I ask a favor?" He paused. "I'm at the Pleasant Valley Steakhouse. Can you bring Crystal over and have her drive Tessa's car to her apartment? She's had an upset and can't drive. I'm taking her to my place." He slipped his arm around Tessa's waist, anchoring her to his side. "Great. Thanks. We're standing by her car."

"Crystal will take your car home."

Tessa rested her head on his shoulder. Before long, Jordan and Crystal arrived. Tessa handed her car keys to her friend and said a quiet thank you. Jordan gave Damon a concerned look, but Damon shook his head.

209

Tessa was quiet the entire drive to his house. Once inside, he put on some water for tea. She liked a cup in the evenings, and tonight she probably needed it.

"I'm sorry," she said softly.

"What are you apologizing for?" he asked.

"Because my brother is an ass." She shook her head. "Why did I think he wanted a nice dinner with his sister? Why did I think he simply wanted to meet you?"

Damon frowned at the despair in her voice.

"Nope," Tessa continued, almost speaking to herself. "I should have guessed he wanted to use it as a photo op. I should have known. It's not like my family really cares about me or my life."

That got Damon's attention. He made her cup of tea and carried it over to her. "I'm sorry your brother is an asshole."

"Opportunist is more like it." She took a sip of her tea. "My mom is a good person, but how she puts up with their dog and pony show, I'll never know."

"Has it always been like this for you?" He sat down next to her and put his arm around her shoulder.

"Sometimes." She set her tea on the side table, curled her feet under her, and leaned against him. Damon slipped his arm down, holding her closer. "When I was little, it wasn't so bad. Of course, kids don't have long attention spans, and my mother wanted me to have a normal childhood."

He heard the irony in her voice. "Your mother tried to shelter you."

"She did. It worked for the most part until I became a teenager." She sighed. "Then Dad wanted me at all the functions. God, I hated them." A shudder shook her body. *"Look at the camera, Tessa. Smile, Tessa. The dress doesn't*

210

look right on her. Oh look, she's dating another boy; what happened to the old boyfriend?"

Damon didn't blame her if tonight was a taste of what she'd been through. "That's why you were upset with the picture in the gossip column."

"Yes. Somehow my father saw it and called me." She tilted her head back and looked up at him. "I need to confess to you: I played down our relationship with my father and brother."

"I gathered that. Why?"

"Because I know both of them. You saw tonight how my brother was questioning you and our relationship."

"I thought at first he was being a good brother."

"Hardly. He wants to make sure there's no dirt that can come back to bite him or my dad in the butt. The thing is, I've protected them all this time, but they seem to have no regard for me."

"How have you protected them?"

She blew out a breath. "Ruthledge is my mother's maiden name. She and Dad got married when they were both nineteen, so I doubt anyone remembers it."

"Why use your mother's maiden name?" He wanted to understand why she did that.

"Because my life was hell in DC, and I wanted to put it behind me." She shifted. "I know we talked, but I never revealed the whole story."

"Will you now?" Had she lied to him? No. She'd answered his questions, but had never elaborated, and he hadn't asked her to.

"Yes, but it's a long story." She sat up. "I left my brother without a place to sleep tonight."

Damon laughed. "I think that's the least of his problems."

"Maybe." She picked up her phone. "Let me check something." She fiddled around on her phone. "Let me send a quick text to my boss. I have enough vacation time; I'm taking tomorrow off." She did what she needed to do then settled back down in his arms.

"Are you okay discussing this tonight?" Her brother's actions had to still be fresh in her head.

"I'm fine. I'd rather get it out now." She paused as if to gather her thoughts, then spoke. "From the time I was about fourteen, my dad wanted me in the spotlight with him, my brother, and mother. I think I told you my dad wanted me to follow in his footsteps."

"You did."

"I hated every second of being in front of the media. If I wore something they didn't like, I got raked over the coals for it. Even in school I was a congressman's daughter, never Tessa."

"That must have been hard." Teenagers were just finding their sense of identity, so to have that stripped from her must have been devastating.

"It was. My mother tried. It's when I got into college and wanted to go my own way that things got really difficult. The lifestyle afforded me an escape."

"I can see that." From what she'd told him, her friends in the lifestyle had protected her and made sure she was safe.

"Not that I didn't enjoy it, but for a little while each week, I could be Tessa, not Congressman Chesterton's daughter." She paused and stared at her hands. "When I rebelled against studying political science and wanted to study library science, my father was not happy, but I told you that."

"Yes." His lips brushed her temple. "I'm glad your

mother fought for you."

"Me too. Anyway, I was doing my master's degree, and I met this guy. Jack." She cleared her throat. "We met at a local coffee shop. I thought he was another student."

"Go on."

"We started talking. He was so nice and friendly. After several meetings at the coffee shop, we went out to dinner. Nothing big, nothing fancy. I was in heaven."

Damon had a feeling this story didn't end happily, but he'd let her get it out.

"Jack met the family, and things went well. I thought, maybe I'd finally found someone who wanted me for me."

"He betrayed you."

"Yes. I found out—mind you, after I was engaged to him—that he was using me to get closer to my father."

"Bastard."

"He was that all right. When I confronted him about it, he didn't deny it. Told me, why not? I wouldn't be able to do anything in DC, not with a congressman for a father and only a lowly Master of Library Science. And I was a freak because I liked my sex a little kinky. He'd have none of that once we were married."

"I hope you told the little bastard where to go."

Tessa laughed. "Oh, I certainly did. I'd had enough. I graduated the next week, packed up my bags, and left for Seattle."

"Why so far away?"

"It's too easy to be recognized in DC and the surrounding areas. My dad was always in the news, and when he started grooming my brother, so was he. I couldn't do anything once people knew my last name."

"So once here, you took your mother's last name."

"I did. With her permission, I had a legal name change.

Best thing I ever did, but now I think it's all ruined."

"Why?"

"That photo of us at the coffee shop and tonight's photo that my brother set up. It will be front-page news tomorrow, and my anonymity will be gone. I'll be thrust right back in the spotlight."

Damon's anger at Tessa's brother rose. Allen knew what he was doing. He'd even admitted it. He used Tessa, but also Damon. Damon really didn't care about himself. He'd run his store long enough and as for his toy making? No one in the lifestyle would care. He was worried about Tessa.

"Is that why you took the day off?"

"Partially. But also because I want to give you some distance."

"Me?" What was she thinking?

"Damon, I can't help but think how this could affect you. Not to mention my friends." She laid her hand over his chest. "You're getting ready to expand your store, and if someone found out about the club, well, I don't want anyone hurt because of me or my family."

She was so selfless. "Sweetheart, I'll be fine."

"But what happens if they boycott your store?"

Damon laughed. "Honey, this is Pleasant Valley. Everyone knows about my store, even the town council who approved it. As for the club, the council knows. I'm sure most of the town knows as well."

"I need to warn everyone." She sat up. "They deserve the courtesy." Tessa fished around for her purse and pulled her cell out.

"Do you want me to call Jordan? Crystal is probably with him."

"No. I should do it." She dialed. "Hey, Sierra, is Max

with you? Good, can you put me on speaker. I'm going to conference Crystal and Jordan in."

Damon stood up and took her now cold tea into the kitchen while she talked to her friends. He could tell from her end of the conversation that her friends were rallying around her. He knew it would happen. They were a tight knit group.

"Well, that's done." She set her phone aside. "I guess I should go home."

"Stay." He sat back down. "Give yourself tonight to absorb and plan." As he finished speaking, her cell rang.

Tessa picked it up and looked at the screen. Damon saw her brother's name. He took the phone from her. "I'm protecting you." He flipped the *on* button. "Allen, Tessa is not ready to speak with you."

"Put my sister on the phone."

"Not going to happen."

"At least let me in the apartment."

Allen's whiny voice irritated Damon's nerves. "She's not there. Go to a hotel for the night."

"But…"

Damon hung up and turned Tessa's phone off. He pulled out his phone and sent a quick text to Max and Jordan, letting them know Tessa's phone was off so her friends wouldn't worry if they tried to reach her.

"I can't believe you did that."

Damon looked at Tessa. She didn't look upset, and her voice was her normal tone.

"As I said, I'm protecting you, even if it is from your own family."

She snuggled up to him. "Thank you. You're right. I need tonight, here, with you."

"So you have it." He relaxed back against the sofa with

her in his arms. Tomorrow they could sort this all out.

* * * *

"Tessa…" Damon started the next morning after breakfast.

"No, Damon. I don't want to involve you more than you're already involved." Her voice was firm. Tessa had to do this on her own. The problem was getting Damon to understand. Yes, she let him take over last night, but now she had to be strong.

She hadn't been wrong about the picture in the paper. Front page, with a long article, not only about her brother, but her father as well, and dinner last night. No mention that she and Damon had left. Just a full article about the visit between Representative Hopper and her brother. Luckily, not much was mentioned about Damon, other than he was a local business owner. Nevertheless, the picture was out there for anyone to see.

Thank goodness the article hadn't mentioned Allen was her brother. That was one silver lining.

"I don't like the idea of dropping you blocks from your apartment."

"I know." She touched his cheek. "But you saw as we drove by, the press was all over my place with my brother holding court. And I don't want you caught up in this."

"I'm a big boy. I can handle it."

Her lips curved up at his indignant tone. "I know you can." She brushed a kiss over his lips. "Please understand, I need to do this myself." While having Damon at her side, fighting her battles, was nice, this was something she had to do.

He shrugged in obvious resignation. "All right. Though I don't like it."

* * * *

"Call me once you're inside your apartment," Damon insisted as he parked two blocks from her apartment.

"I will."

"You better." He grasped the back of her head and pulled her in for a kiss.

Tessa relaxed into his hold and his kiss. He couldn't guess her intentions. Oh, she'd call him to let him know she was home, but until this all blew over, she wasn't going to see him. She wasn't going to risk any backlash on him, his business, or the club.

He broke the kiss, but his hand lingered. "I'm going to miss you."

"I'll miss you too." That was the truth. When he removed his hand, she opened the door and slipped out of the vehicle.

She turned back to him. "I care about you, Damon. No matter what anyone says. I do care." She shut the door and rushed down the sidewalk, blinking back the tears. When she turned onto the street for her apartment complex, she sighed at the chaos.

Tessa lifted her chin and walked into the fray. Reporters shouted questions and flashes went off, but she ignored everyone, including her brother, and marched straight up to her apartment. Thank goodness the front door had finally been fixed.

Her brother trailed behind her and followed her through the door. She slammed the door and threw the locks. She'd probably have to find a new place to live now.

"How dare you walk out on me last night and leave me without a place to stay," her brother ranted, all traces of his media smile gone.

"You look no worse for wear." His suit was freshly pressed, and he looked like he'd slept.

"That's not the point."

Tessa set her purse down after taking out her cell phone. "What is the point, Allen? You set me up last night. None of this was about spending time with me, your sister. It was all about politics." She put her phone on the table and turned to look at her brother. "Pack up and go to a hotel for the rest of your stay."

"What? You're kicking me out?"

"I am." She'd had enough. "I love you, Allen, I love Dad, too, and Mom. But I'm out of the politics. I don't want the limelight or to be thrust into the political situations again. It's better if you leave."

"I can't believe this." Allen drew a hand through his perfectly combed hair.

"Believe it. I don't want this. None of it. You can bask in the attention at a hotel, or giving interviews at the local park, but not where I live. Not my sanctuary." But it was no longer that. Her lips twitched, thinking about the club. Wicked Sanctuary. Max had named it aptly.

"Fine." Her brother stomped to the spare bedroom.

Tessa shook her head. Step one done. It was hard, but she did it. She picked her cell up. "Hey, I'm home."

"How bad is it?" Damon asked.

"Bad."

"Okay. What did you mean by your last words?"

She'd hoped he wouldn't ask. "I need some space." More like time to figure her way out of this mess with the press.

"Tessa." His voice deepened, and Tessa found herself sitting down before she fell. That deep husky tone of his did it to her every time.

"Damon, please, don't make this any harder." Her heart was already shattering. But she needed to do this for her own sake and for their relationship. She had to protect Damon and her friends. To prove to herself she was strong enough to handle anything thrown at her.

"I'm not giving up on us."

"I'm not either." She wanted him to understand that.

"I mean it, Tessa. I won't let you climb into a hole. You'll be hearing from me." The line went dead.

Now what did he mean? Tessa looked up when she heard her brother.

"You know Dad won't be happy about this."

"I really don't care." She was going to remain firm about this and not be guilt tripped into anything.

"Fine." Allen marched to the front door with his suitcase. "I do love you, sis."

Damn. Tessa walked over to him. "I love you too, baby brother." She gave him a hug and a kiss. "Remember to be true to you."

"I will." He hugged her back, then broke the embrace. He opened the door, walked out, and closed it behind him.

Tessa could hear the reporters shouting through the window when Allen walked outside. Not their words, not that she cared. Right now, she needed to figure out her life and what she was going to do.

* * * *

"I'm at a loss," Damon said to Max and Jordan Friday night. He'd left messages for Tessa, texted her. Nothing came back but a couple of emojis. Those emojis gave him hope. Mainly because they were hugs and smiles.

"Why do women retreat like this?" Jordan asked.

"Because they need time to figure things out, and they get scared, just like we do," Max said.

"But it never takes us much time to figure things out." Damon paced around the club classroom. They'd met early tonight to discuss the plans on expanding the club with Zeke and how it could be done with minimal disruption.

"Women are wired differently," Max said.

"They sure are," Jordan agreed. "Crystal goes into another room whenever Tessa calls."

Damon blew out a breath. "I want to see Tessa, but at the same time, I'm afraid she'll shut me out completely if I do."

"That sounds familiar," Jordan said.

"Another one bites the dust," Max commented.

Damon stared at them. "What are you two talking about?"

His friends laughed.

"Buddy,"—Max clapped him on the shoulder—"you're head over heels in love with Tessa."

Damon was about to deny it, but realized he couldn't. "Well, yeah… I guess I am." When had that happened? Didn't matter. What if he lost her? No, he wouldn't allow that to happen. He was done playing it safe.

"Welcome to our world," Jordan said.

"What do I do now?"

"I'd say go after her," Max started. "But in this case, give her a little more time. Based on what you've told us, and what I pried out of Sierra, Tessa's family is the issue. Not you."

"She thinks she's protecting me and the club."

"Of course, she does," Jordan said. "Crystal thought the same way."

"But you didn't let her," Damon said.

"No, but our situation was different," Jordan reminded him.

Jordan was right. His and Crystal's situation was more around the lawsuit and threats than press and political pressure. Not that Tessa bent to pressure. He'd seen on the news how the press stayed outside her apartment until her brother emerged explaining that he was giving his sister some space and privacy. Yeah, that was a joke.

"I'll give her until the end of this weekend, then it's gloves off."

* * * *

"Son of a bitch." The words slipped out of Damon's mouth when he opened Sunday's paper to the local scene page. That damn gossip reporter was at it again, but this time, she actually put it together.

Damon Kline is the mystery man in Tessa Ruthledge's life. As you know, Ms. Ruthledge is the daughter of prominent congressman, Rep. Russell Chesterton, I-MD2. This reporter smelled a story when she took a picture of the couple with their friends a few weeks ago. Now that I've been able to do some digging, Mr. Kline owns Klineman's, a local adult store. Although this reporter will tell you that it's a very tasteful looking store.

Mr. Kline has also purchased the empty store front next to his adult store. Maybe he's going to expand. A little further digging and I found out that Mr. Kline designs and manufactures adult toys. One has to wonder what else Mr. Kline does.

And does Ms. Ruthledge know about his peculiar activities? Keep watch on this column because there will be more to come.

The paper crinkled under Damon's fingers. Damn nosy reporter. He picked up his cell and called Destiny to warn her. She laughed and asked him if he minded if she had a little fun. Tasteful fun. He told her to go for it.

He knew Destiny wouldn't do anything to harm him or the business, but maybe it was time to shake things up a

221

little bit more. His next call was to Max and Jordan to warn them. They both laughed and said at least he got better press than Jordan did.

Leave it to his friends to yank him out of his anger. He called Tessa. It went directly to voicemail. "Tessa, sweetheart, I know you don't read the paper, but you might need to look at today's local scene page. I don't want you to worry. Call me."

The second he hung up, his phone rang. "Hello."

"Destiny here. You better get to the store."

"What happened?" Damon was already crossing the room to grab his keys and wallet.

"Reporters everywhere."

"Keep the store closed." Thank goodness they had a rear entrance. "I'll be there in thirty."

Damon jumped into his car. Destiny wasn't kidding. He pulled into the parking lot, figuring it would be better if he confronted this head on.

"Mr. Kline," reporters shouted as he climbed out of his vehicle.

Damon held his hands up, and they quieted. "Listen folks, it's Sunday morning. You're trespassing. I'm asking all of you to leave."

"Freedom of the press," someone yelled.

"I agree, but only so long as it doesn't hinder my business." Damon pushed his way through them to the storefront. Destiny opened the door for him, then shut and locked it.

Damon started laughing when he saw her. She was wearing a corset, black skirt, fishnet stockings, and sneakers.

"Hey, it's comfortable."

"Destiny, you need a raise." He gave her a hug. Flashes

went off. Damon groaned, and Destiny stuck her tongue out at the reporters.

Damon pulled out his cell and made a call. "Officer Wolfe."

"Hey, Logan, it's Damon."

"What can I do for you?"

"I've got a bunch of reporters in front of the store. Anything you can do?"

"Let me send a couple of patrol cars around. Are they blocking the entrance and sidewalk?"

"Yep."

"Okay, we have ordinances against that."

"Thanks, Logan." He hung up and looked at Destiny. "The police should be here to get rid of this unruly bunch. I'm going to take inventory."

"Taking my job?"

Damon laughed. "Nope, but I might as well be helpful while I'm here." It would help take his mind off of Tessa and the fact she hadn't called him back.

Forty minutes later, the sidewalk and the front of the store had been cleared. Not that the reporters had left; now they were across the street. Destiny unlocked the front door. Two officers walked in.

"Thank you," Damon said striding up to them.

"You're welcome. Is it okay if we look around? We are on our lunch break."

"Fine with me."

Destiny wiggled her eyebrows, and Damon shook his head. Now that the reporters had been forced away, customers entered the shop. Damon was glad to help Destiny as they got busy for a while, then it settled down.

Even after the police left, the reporters kept their distance. Damon was glad for that. He finished up inventory, then grabbed a couple of chairs and took them to the front of the store. "Come sit down for a minute, Destiny."

Destiny stared at him as she took a seat. "Am I fired?"

"Hell, no. I can't fire you." He was honest. Destiny helped him so much. "I wanted to clue you in on my plans for the store."

"Are you going to sell it?"

Damon blinked. "Where is this coming from?"

"Well, between the stuff I read in the paper and the reporters, I wouldn't blame you."

"I'm not selling it. Far from it." He spread his hands out. "I bought the empty store next door."

"I read about that."

"The book club has become very popular, and we don't have the room here for the amount of books I know you'd like us to carry."

"True. I really want to carry more on the lifestyle. People are always asking, and we have to order them."

"Right." He'd seen the uptick in book sales. "So I figured the next door space could be used for the book club and as a book store. And I want you to run it as my manager."

Destiny's jaw dropped open. "This is the last thing I expected."

"You're a great employee. I'll be hiring more people since we seem to be getting busier."

"I bet we will after all this press."

"You think so?"

"Look at this morning. Sundays are slow, which is why I do inventory then. Not today. Damon, people aren't as prudish as we think." She looked up. "Speaking of which…"

SEDUCE

Damon glanced up. "Mr. Mayor and the town council," he greeted them as he stood up.

"Damon," the mayor said, shaking his hand. "We thought we'd stop by and offer our support."

"I really appreciate it." Maybe Destiny was right.

"Yes, and I'd love to hear more about your book club?" one of the female council members said.

"I'd love to chat about it," Destiny said. "Anyone else?" Several members followed Destiny.

* * * *

Tessa closed her eyes when someone pounded on her apartment door Monday night. Work had been a challenge today. At least the reporters had stopped hanging around, though this new gossip column was sure to bring them back to her doorstep.

"Tessa, you open this door right now."

Shit. She jumped up, unlocked the door, and opened it. Her father swept by her along with his chief of staff. "What are you doing here, Father?"

"I've come to save you."

"What?" She barely prevented herself from rolling her eyes.

"I saw the article about that man you're dating."

"It's old news." At least she hoped it was, but the article yesterday made her doubt it.

"I'm not talking about the one with your brother. I'm taking the one that was in yesterday's paper. What are you thinking, dating someone like that?"

"Like what?" She put her hands on her hips. "Damon is a good man." He was. He was the man she loved. Tessa froze. When had she'd fallen in love with Damon? She almost laughed out loud. Loving him had snuck up on her, and for the first time in a very long time, she trusted in that love and in Damon.

"You told me there wasn't anything between you."

Her father's voice brought her out of her musings. She had, but the relationship had been so new. "It doesn't matter."

"It does. Pack a bag."

"What?" Her head was spinning.

"I'm taking you to my hotel where I can protect you. Tomorrow, at my press conference, you will denounce this man and his business."

"Like hell." She wasn't going to leave her apartment with her father.

"Don't talk like that." He grabbed her arm. "Let's go. Perry can pack your clothes."

"No." She pulled away. There was a knock at her door. "Now who?" This time, she looked out the peephole and opened the door.

"Tessa." Sierra enveloped her in a hug.

"Inside, honey," Max said.

Sierra shifted so they were inside, and Max closed the door.

"Who are these people?" her father demanded.

Max's eyebrows rose at her father's tone. "Max Preston, Mr. Chesterton."

"How does he know?" Tessa whispered to Sierra. There was no way they decided dropped by.

"Max has spies."

While Tessa should have been surprised, she wasn't. Max was good at knowing what was going on. Tessa almost giggled.

"This is Tessa's best friend and my girlfriend, Sierra."

Tessa's father huffed out a breath. "Tessa, a moment alone."

"It's okay," she told Sierra. "The spare bedroom will have to do." She wasn't letting her father in her bedroom. He followed her down the short hall and into the room.

"I'm having a press conference tomorrow at city hall. You will be there and denounce this Damon person."

"We've been over this."

"Be there or I'll ruin his life." With that, her father stormed out of the room—the slamming of the door telling her they were gone.

"Tessa," Sierra called.

Tessa walked back into the family room and stared at her friends. "I need help," she said. She had a plan in mind, but she was going to need to talk to Damon first.

"Tell us what we can do," Max said.

"Not here." She felt like the walls had ears. She was also sure reporters were going to be camped on her doorstep once again. "Can I come crash at your place for a day or two?" She'd go over everything that had happened with them first.

"Let's pack you a bag." Sierra took her by the arm and led her into her bedroom.

* * * *

Two hours later, she'd explained everything not only to Max and Sierra, but to Crystal and Jordan as well.

"Well, damn. I thought my family was messed up," Crystal said.

"I think mine takes top place." Tessa felt better than she had a few hours ago. Being here with her friends, talking things out. She had some very big decisions to make.

"Any legal options?" Max asked Jordan.

"Coercion, but hard to prove," Jordan said.

"Can we stop the press conference?" Sierra asked.

"Not a chance," Tessa muttered.

"Might be an unpopular opinion at the moment," Max said. "Tessa, you need to talk to Damon."

"I do." She stared at her feet. She wanted to see him so badly, but she had decided to wait. He'd called her yesterday to warn her about the article. Who knew a tiny gossip article could create such a stir? Now, her father was going to make an even bigger spectacle of her life. Yeah, she needed to talk to Damon.

"I'll call him to come over," Max said.

"No offense, but I really need privacy to talk to him," Tessa said. "I have some ideas how I might fix this, but Damon will play a big part in it."

"We'll go over to the club while you talk," Sierra said.

"I can't kick you out of your house." No, if she was going to do this. She was going to do it right. "Max, would you drive me to Damon's house?"

"Sure. Do I warn Damon?"

"I'd rather surprise him."

"Works for me."

Tessa stood and grabbed her overnight bag. She could always bring it back with her if things didn't work out with Damon.

Tessa ran every option over in her head as Max drove her to Damon's. There were far too few choices. She wanted to make the right one. What if Damon didn't want to talk to her? She tangled her fingers together. He was the one who'd called her about the article and kept calling and texting her. He'd talk to her. She blinked when she realized Max had stopped in front of Damon's house.

"Call when you're ready for us to come over. If Damon refuses, I'll come over and kick his dumb ass," Max said as Tessa climbed out of his SUV.

"Thanks, Max. I don't think kicking him will be necessary." Tessa shut the door. Taking a deep breath, she walked up to the house and rang the bell.

A minute later, the door was pulled open. "Tessa, oh thank god." He pulled her into his arms.

"Damon, what's going on?" The panic in his voice made her heart pound.

He pulled her into the house and pushed the door closed with his foot.

"Where is your phone?"

"Right here." She opened her purse and pulled it out, then groaned at the missed calls from Damon. "I'm sorry I've had it on silent. Things have been crazy."

"You could say that." He framed her face with his hands. "Are you okay, sweetheart?"

"I am now." And that was the truth. His embrace did more for her than her friends' hugs.

"Let me take that." He took her bag from her hand and set it on the floor. "Come on into the family room."

Tessa slipped off her shoes, left her purse next to her bag, and took her phone with her. Damon sat down on the sofa and pulled her into his lap.

"I need to hold you," he said.

"I'm sorry I worried you." She was. It was the last thing she wanted to do.

"I was about to call Sierra and Crystal."

"I wished you would have. I was with them." She brushed the hair away from his face. "So much has happened."

"No matter what, I'm here for you. I mean that."

"I know." She blew out a breath. "Thanks for the heads up on the article. I hope it didn't cause you any issues."

"More business, actually."

"Oh that's good." She was happy for him. Now came the hard part. "My father showed up at my apartment tonight."

Damon stiffened. "I take it he wasn't happy."

"No." She laid her hand on his cheek. "He wants me to denounce you at a press conference tomorrow."

Damon held her gaze. "I know you'll handle it."

His trust in her hit her in the gut. So much trust. "I love you so much." The words flowed out of her. This man would never betray her, only support her and keep her safe.

"Tessa?" His eyes grew bright with need.

"I mean it, Damon. I love you. I have no intention of denouncing you. No matter what my father says. But he's vowed to ruin you. I can't allow that. We're stuck. I don't know how to stop him from trying to ruin you, and I refuse to give you up."

Damon leaned down and rubbed his nose against hers.

"So we're going to beat him at his own game."

"What do you mean?" he asked.

"Let me call Max, Sierra, Crystal, and Jordan and see if they're willing to burn the midnight oil with us. I have an idea, but we'll need help. Would you mind getting coffee going and some snacks?"

"Anything for you." He moved her onto the sofa, leaned down, and brushed his lips over hers. "It will be fine."

"I hope so, because I'm tired of this limbo." She called Sierra. She had a feeling it was going to be a long night, but she was hopeful Damon and her friends were on her side. They would help her.

CHAPTER TWELVE

"This is crazy," Tessa said the next afternoon as they parked at city hall. They'd discussed her plan last night. Her gut tightened at what she had to do. And she had an ace in the hole if her father persisted.

"It's perfect." Damon turned to her. "Never forget that I love you, and your father can't ruin me."

Tessa's jaw dropped open. "You love me?" Even though he hadn't said it back last night, she didn't expect him to.

"I do." He got out and opened her door, taking her hand. "Together?" Tessa nodded.

Hand in hand, they walked to the front steps of city hall where the press was already gathered, a podium set up with microphones attached to it. Her father was talking about Damon and his businesses.

"Damn him," Tessa muttered.

"You can do this," Damon whispered.

"As long as you're by my side, I can do anything." Her father frowned when he saw them approach. Damon let go of Tessa's hand and stayed off to the side, but close enough that he could get to her if she needed him.

"And here is my daughter," her father announced holding out his hand.

Breathe, Tessa reminded herself. She walked up to the podium. "Hello. I'm sorry you all wasted your afternoon. But there is really nothing for me to say." Tessa squinted as the sun hit her in the eyes, and she saw her friends off to the side. Turning her head slightly, she saw Damon. "Damon is a good man who runs two very legitimate businesses, both approved by the town council and, frankly, both thriving. I'm sorry my father can't see through his own prejudice. That's all I have to say."

She stepped away. Her father started sputtering. "He's brainwashed my daughter. The man is nothing but a pornographer."

"Excuse me," another strong male voice spoke out.

Tessa watched as a young man walked up to the podium. "For those of you who don't know me, I'm Congressman Potts. I represent this district, and I'm here to show my support for Damon Kline."

The reporters erupted along with her father. Potts held his hands up. "I understand Congressman Chesterton wants to sully Mr. Kline's reputation, so I want to inform you of some facts." He pulled a piece of paper out of his pocket. "Mr. Kline's business not only brings in tax revenue, but he is a well-liked businessman. Many people don't know this about him, but Mr. Kline is our top donor for the city parks, our local kids center, and he's also part of Friends of the Library."

Tessa squeezed Damon's hand, and he glanced down at her. "You are?" she whispered.

"Yes. I prefer to keep it quiet, but in this case, I think it's appropriate."

"For anyone who hasn't been inside Mr. Kline's store, I encourage you to visit. It's not some sleazy place as Congressman Chesterton tries to characterize it. It's a very tasteful store. Mr. Kline's store also runs a local book club every month that has become quite popular."

"He does," someone in the crowd yelled. "I love it."

"It's great," another voice said.

"Thank you," Potts said. "So as you can see, Mr. Kline

is a good citizen, and I am glad he's part of our town."

"What about his toy-making business?" a female reporter yelled. Tessa recognized that voice.

Damon squeezed her hand before going up to the podium. "I have several degrees in engineering. I make adult toys for those who choose to use them. I don't sell to anyone under eighteen, and before you ask, I do that by asking for ID that shows age, but not only that, they must pay by credit card in their name. Not many under eighteen have credit cards."

"Mr. Kline, why did you pick adult toys and store?"

"Because it's time for adult sexuality to come out of the closet, so to speak. We're all human beings, and we are—for the most part—sexual beings as well. It's our own business how we explore our sexuality, but I would prefer to be open about it."

There was a small cheer, then the mayor came huffing up the stairs. "I, as mayor, and the town council"—the mayor waved his hand—"stand behind Mr. Kline. I believe Congressman Chesterton is trying to stir up trouble where there is none."

"He's taking my daughter down a sinner's path."

"Oh, for goodness sake." Tessa marched up to her father. "Quit with all the preacher talk. Maybe you should remember what happened when I was sixteen." With that, she turned to Damon. Reporters started yelling questions.

Damon took her hand and raised it to his lips. Tessa smiled, and they walked away.

* * * *

"I'm dying of curiosity here, what did your father do when you were sixteen?" Sierra asked as all of them were at Damon's house celebrating.

"I caught my father cheating on my mother." Tessa's

233

mother knew and had forgiven her father, but Tessa never really had. "Hearing him today with all his bluster and crap, I couldn't take it anymore."

Her cell rang; it was her mother. "I need to take this." Tessa stood up and walked outside on the patio. "Hey, Mom."

"I've left your father."

Tessa wobbled on her feet. "Oh my God, Mom. If what I said had anything to do with it—"

"It wasn't what you said, my darling Tessa. I've been fed up with your father for a while now. That's why I put my foot down when you wanted to get your master's. Why I encouraged you to move away and take my maiden name. What he intended to do and has done to you and your nice young man was the last straw."

"Mom, what are you going to do?" Tessa was worried. Her mother had married straight out of high school. She'd always been a wife and mother and in politics and the public eye.

"I'm going up to New Hampshire to live with my sister for a while. I wanted you to know because the crap is going to hit the fan. I didn't want you caught unaware."

"Thanks, Mom. Call me when you get to Auntie's house."

"I will, baby. Maybe once everything is calmed down, I'll come out to Washington to visit you and your young man."

"That would be great, Mom."

"Love you, baby girl."

"Love you too, Mom." Tessa went back inside. Damon was at her side in a second.

"Is everything okay? You've got that stunned look on your face."

"My mom is divorcing my father." Tessa smiled. "Life is grand."

* * * *

It was after ten when everyone finally left. Tessa helped Damon clean up and then Damon led her into his bedroom.

"It's been a long week, hasn't it?" he said as he began undressing her.

"It has." Tessa let Damon do this for her. He'd been so supportive, so there for her. "I love you so much, Damon."

"I love you too, my Tessa."

"I am yours."

"And I belong to you." He stared at her. "On the bed, I have a surprise for you."

Tessa did as Damon asked, wondering what he had planned. She kept her gaze on him, and when he turned from the closet, she burst out laughing. "Oh no, the big bad wolf, are you going to eat me?

Damon had on the wolf mask from the Valentine's Day party. "Why yes, my dear. I'm going to eat you in a way that will give you pleasure."

He pounced.

Other books by Marie Tuhart

Her Desert Prince (Desert Destiny)
Her Desert Doctor (Desert Destiny)
Her Desert Horseman (Desert Destiny)
Her Desert Protector (Desert Destiny)
Highland Dom (McMillan Passion)
Bound & Teased
Claimed by the Sheikh
Billionaire's Cowboy's Conquest
More of You (Club Crave)
Reflections of you (Club Crave)
Bound to Love You (Club Crave)
Hot for You (Club Crave)
Tempt (Wicked Sanctuary Series)
Entice (Wicked Sanctuary Series)

Coming Summer 2021 – Ravish (Wicked Sanctuary Series)
Coming Fall 2021 – Possess (Wicked Sanctuary Series)

ABOUT THE AUTHOR

Marie Tuhart lives in the beautiful Pacific Northwest. She loves to read and write, and when she's not writing, she spends time with her two dogs, Tommy and Trina, family, traveling and enjoying life.

Marie is a multi-published author with The Wild Rose Press and Trifecta Publishing, and is self-published. To be alerted to her new releases, you can join Marie's newsletter on her website: www.mairetuhart.com

Ravish – A Wicked Sanctuary Novel - Prevew

Lara Meyer rolled her eyes as she made her way out from behind the counter of her cafe Sweet and Savory. Her brother Keith, and her ex-husband, Walter stood near the bikers having lunch.

"Keith, Walter, stop bothering my customers and leave."

Both men turned to her. "They're nothing but scum and thieves," her brother said.

The bikers stiffened. "Oh grow up." She got between her brother, ex and the bikers.

"These men," her brother sneered, "will get you closed down faster than rats."

"The only rats I see are the two standing in front of me." Damn she had no idea why her brother and ex seemed to hate the bikers.

"We're not the ones making trouble," Walter said putting a hand on her shoulder.

She stiffened, trying to tamp down the instant fear that swept over her. *It's okay.* She reminded herself. He couldn't do anything here. Lara stepped away so her ex's hand fell away. One of the bikers stood up and Lara feared there would be a fight. "Enough." Lara pushed her brother and ex in the chest making them fall back two steps. She turned her head. "I'm okay, Monty," she told the biker. He was a big guy.

"Fine, but if you need us, yell." He sat back down.

The door to the cafe opened and Lara almost let out a groan. Colby Durham, owner of Durham's Leather shop, strode in. His raven hair mussed and his green eyes assessing. The bikers frequented his shop and most of the time then came to her cafe for food. She hadn't been sure of the group in the beginning or of Colby's shop, but the past few months had improved her business and there'd never been a lick of trouble until now.

Not that Lara minded the increase in business, but every time she saw Colby her heart sped up a little. She didn't have time for men, especially ones that made her think of all the naughty things they could do to each other.

"Problem?" Colby asked as he strode over to her.

"Nothing that I can't handle." Lara huffed. She didn't want him involved. Her brothers and ex were always in here making comments, but this was the first time they did it with a table full of bikers. The last thing she wanted was a fight to break out.

Colby nodded, then took a seat with the bikers.

"Time for you two to leave," Lara said.

"Not until they do," her brother said.

Lara swore silently. "They are having lunch, while you two are doing nothing but making a scene." She fought her temper down, it wouldn't do to lose it in front of all her customers in the café.

The door opened again. Who called the police? She looked over at the counter where her employee, Eve, nodded. At least one of them was thinking straight.

"See, the police are here to arrest the riff-raff," Keith said.

"The only riff-raff is you," Lara shot back.

"Officer Logan Wolfe, what seems to be the problem."

"The problem is those bikers," Walter said waving his hand at them.

"Officer Wolfe, the bikers are not the problem. These

239

two are." She pointed her finger at her brother and her ex. "They've come into my cafe making accusations about customers just minding their own business, and they won't leave."

"I see." The officer looked over her brother an ex. "Gentlemen if you'd please come outside with me."

"Do you know who I am?" Her brother puffed out his chest.

"Actually, I do, Mr. Meyer."

Colby stood up and looked at the officer. "Officer Wolfe, if you need a witness, the two men here were harassing the bikers when I came in." Colby's voice was calm and Lara found herself relaxing for the first time since her brother and ex walked in.

"Of course there is and you're part of it," Keith said. "Your leather shop is bringing in a criminal element."

"Oh for goodness sake, Keith. These men are not criminals and neither is Colby."

"I don't think you realize," Keith went on ignoring her completely. "I can ruin you all."

Lara's temper flared. She hated it when her family flaunted their wealth. That was one of the reasons she had very little to do with them. "You might, but do you have enough money for all the lawsuits that will be coming your way. Especially the one from me?"

"All right," Officer Wolfe said. "That's enough. Outside Mr. Meyer, and you too." Office Wolfe pointed at Walter. "Now." His tone hard.

Keith glared at her. "Very well." He turned and marched to toward the door.

"This isn't over," Walter muttered as he followed.

Lara clasped her hands together so no one would see them shaking. She hated confrontation. But she wasn't about to let her brother and ex drive away her customers. She turned to the bikers.

"I'm sorry guys."

"Not your fault," the biker who stood to defend her earlier said.

"Please stay as long as you want, and I'll have Eve refill your beverages," Lara turned and Colby was right there.

"Are you okay?" he asked, his green eyes filled with concern.

"I'm fine. Just angry." Angry and scared. Confrontation wasn't her strong suit, but she wasn't about to let anyone harass her customers. She marched away and went behind the counter. She saw Colby grab and empty chair and sit down to talk to the bikers. "Eve, please refill their drinks and see if Mr. Durham wants anything. On the house."

"Sure thing." Eve sauntered out from behind the counter.

Lara kept a smile on her face as customers began to show up and order. At least this had happened before the lunchtime rush or the entire town would have seen what happened. She almost laughed, since she was sure it was already making news on the gossip tree.

She glanced out the front window of her cafe to see Officer Wolfe talking with Keith and Walter. Yep, she was pretty sure her aunt Tammy would hear all about this before long.

Lara kept smiling for customer after customer. Office Logan walked back in and talked with Colby and the bikers, then came to the counter. She explained her side of the story, and he told her not to hesitate to call if she needed them.

A little while later, she did see the bikers left. Colby switched to a smaller table as Eve hustled over to the now empty table to wipe it off. It was hardly necessary. Those guys always cleaned up after themselves.

It was after one when the lunch rush started to subside and Lara could draw a deep breath. You'd think she'd be used to it, but today it seemed busier than normal. Maybe it was time to get more help in here. Well, she did have Megan, her other employee. Time to see if they could work out a better schedule.

"I'm going to do refills on coffee," Lara told Eve as she picked up the two carafes. One regular, one decaf and she made her way around the cafe refilling cups as needed. That's when she saw Colby sitting at a table by the window.

"More coffee?" she asked.

"Yes, please. Regular." His deep voice sent a shiver of awareness over her skin.

She poured his coffee and was about to turn away when he spoke again.

"Thank you for protecting my friends." He paused. "Who were the two idiots."

"My brother and my ex, and you don't have to thank me. The bikers are good guys."

"I'm a good guy, too." He grinned at her.

"Jury is still out on that." She walked away, but a smile teased her lips. While Colby might raise her blood pressure in a good way, she didn't need a man in her life.

The cafe door opened, and Sierra and Max breezed through the doorway. "Lara," Sierra called out making a beeline for the counter. Max saw Colby and walked over to him and sit down.

Sierra and her friends, Crystal and Tessa came to the cafe all the time. Heck Crystal stopped by here most mornings for coffee and breakfast.

"Hi Sierra, what can I do you for you today?"

"Do you have a minute to chat?"

"Sure." The lunch rush was gone so she had a little time. "Eve, I'll be right back." Lara slipped out from behind the counter and led Sierra over to an empty table. She couldn't help but glance over at Max and Colby. A rush of heat filled her veins. Two different, yet alike men. They both had that...dominant...that was the only word that fit. A dominant air to them.

"What did you want to talk about?" Lara asked turning her attention back to Sierra.

"I was wondering if you'd be willing to cater an event at the club?"

Lara stared at Sierra. She was aware, as was most of the town about Wicked Sanctuary. After the press conference two weeks ago involving Tessa and Damon it was all people were talking about.

"It depends on what level of catering you're looking for." Most of her food was for quick lunches and snacks.

"Nothing big. Mainly appetizer and desserts."

Lara pulled her phone out of her pocket and brought up the note pad. "That's doable. Do you know what you're looking for?"

"Your Mac & Cheese bites for sure, I would say at least two or three more appetizers or like that, then for desserts, how about brownies, cookies and those lovely mini cupcakes."

She made notes. "Would you like some fruit cups for those who don't want sweets?"

"Oh yes, that would be nice."

"How many people?"

Sierra frowned. "I'd have to ask Max for an exact

count but I would say at least fifty, maybe seventy-five."

"Okay. I gel chafing fuel to keep the food warm."

"We have a strict fire code at the club."

"I understand. I'll make sure it's safe." She ran items through her head. Big metal pans to hold the food, holders, fuel, tongs, plates, napkins. "Is there electrical outlets in the club?"

"I think so." Sierra let out a sigh. "I've never really looked."

"I'll make a note to ask Max. I have a couple of hot boxes that I can keep extra food warm in. This way we don't have to worry about anything going bad."

"Makes sense."

"When is this party?"

Sierra dipped her head. "Ummm, Saturday."

"It's a good thing today is Monday." Gave her time to order what she needed and Saturday to get it all ready.

"Sorry. Max decided on the small party just yesterday."

"No worries. I've worked with less time." Lara smiled. She'd been curious about the club for a while now, so at least she'd get to see the inside of it. Lara glanced over at Max and Colby. She wondered if Colby played?

What was she thinking? She was aware of the lifestyle and even dabbled a bit when she was in college, but since coming home... She'd been to a munch or two, but nothing else. When the club opened, she'd just married Walter. "Bad mistake," she muttered.

"Sorry, I missed that," Sierra said.

Lara shook her head. "I was thinking out loud. Once I get a firm number of people I can do some number crunching for you and let you know about the costs. Then I can get a standard contract drawn up for Max to sign."

"That sounds good."

"What sounds good?" Max asked striding up to the table.

Lara watched Colby open the door to leave, but at the last second he looked back. Their gazes met and he winked. Lara lowered her eyes as her face grew warm.

"Lara agreed to do the party. She'll get a cost for us and if we agree, then a contract."

"Perfect. Thank you, Lara."

"Not a problem. Who were you using for catering before now?" Lara did a little here and there, but she always like to hear who was her competition so to speak.

Max pulled out a chair and sat down. "Usually we don't cater our parties. We might have some fruit and veggies, but that's about it."

"Then why now?" Lara was curious.

"We wanted to try something new. A members only party with food. I do have some pretty strict rules about where the food can be."

"Understandable." Lara started running the menu through her head.

"Also I'll need you to sigh an NDA for the club," Max said.

"Oh?" That was a surprise.

"Yes, as I said, strict rules," Max smiled.

"Can you email it to me?" Lara asked.

"Will do? Anything else you need to know?" he asked.

They talked for another ten minutes. Lara got the information she needed about the electrical outlets, and the number of people. She gave him a rough idea of the cost. Max told her to just email him the contract, the price wasn't an issue. He also advised her if she could arrive a little early on Saturday, so he could show her the area where he wanted to food.

After they left, Lara began cleaning off tables and wiping them down. Eve left at two-thirty, and Lara was putting things away when Colby walked back in.

"Good, I caught you before you closed for the day," he said striding up to the counter.

"What can I do for you?" She almost rolled her eyes at her own question.

"I wanted to know if you've had any trouble with the bikers?"

Lara tilted her head. "No, they're all really good customers. Never a problem. Is this about this morning?"

"A little. I was worried, not so much about the guys from this morning, but that other bikers might be causing you trouble and if so, I'd talk with them."

"No, they're fine. The trouble makers were my brother and my ex."

"Ex?" His eyebrows rose.

"Ex-husband. Four years now, thank goodness."

"Sounds like there's a story there."

"A long and boring one."

"You could never tell a boring story." He leaned against the counter. "I'm glad the guys aren't causing you any issues. They really enjoy your food."

"They do?" Lara stared at Colby. The bikers came in and ordered the same things most days.

"Do you know how many places carry gluten free or wheat free food?"

Lara paused. "Doesn't everyone?"

Colby laughed and a tingle of awareness invaded her veins. "No. Plus you have sugar free desserts and fruit thingies."

"Fruit thingies?" A giggle escaped her lips.

"You know those little cup things that look like

miniature waffle cones."

"Oh, the tart shells."

"Let alone you also have vegetarian options."

"I never realized." She'd added those items to the menu when people started asking her for them.

"So if you ever have any problems with them come get me or better yet, call me." He turned her order pad around and wrote his number. "I mean it. If you ever need me give me a call. That's my cell."

Her belly clenched. Oh, did he do midnight booty calls? Lara closed her eyes. How would it feel to have his hands skim over her belly, as she buried her fingers in his black hair. Okay, she'd been reading way too many erotic romance novels lately. Her mind was running away with her body's needs.

"I will. If I need you." Was that her breathless voice?

"Good. Be safe. See you Saturday night." He sauntered out of the cafe.

Lara locked the door and flipped the neon sign off, then paused. Did he say he'd see her Saturday night? He did. Her heart fluttered. Now she really had a reason to look forward to Saturday night.

CPSIA information can be obtained
at www.ICGtesting.com
Printed in the USA
BVHW040407130721
611731BV00019B/598